## Praise for *Iris a*



"Breathless, eerie,
redemptive trajectory of mental health recovery
instead passes the mic to the ghosts, asking: If your treatment-resistant depression could write its own spiritual autobiography, what would it say? Golems, ancestors, lovers, and psychiatrists are part of the chorus. A penetrating queer story that refuses to settle or resolve its lessons, choosing instead the greatest gift: transformation."
—Alex Leslie, author of *We All Need to Eat*

"*Iris and the Dead* is an unsettling story of an exploitative relationship, blurred boundaries, intergenerational trauma, a fraught medical system, and the shifting landscape of mental illness and recovery. This moving and meditative queer coming-of-age tale is written in lyrical prose vignettes that embrace desire, menace, and myth. Miranda Schreiber's debut is as fierce as it is mesmerizing. A gorgeous book that will appeal to readers of Carmen Maria Machado and Daisy Johnson."
—Kathryn Mockler, author of *Anecdotes*

# IRIS AND THE DEAD

## MIRANDA SCHREIBER

BOOK*HUG PRESS
TORONTO 2025

FIRST EDITION


Library and Archives Canada Cataloguing in Publication

Title: Iris and the dead / Miranda Schreiber.
Names: Schreiber, Miranda, author.
Identifiers: Canadiana (print) 20240524322 | Canadiana (ebook) 20240526422
  ISBN 9781771669290 (softcover)
  ISBN 9781771669306 (EPUB)
Subjects: LCGFT: Novels.
Classification: LCC PS8637.C5648 I75 2025 | DDC C813/.6—dc23

The production of this book was made possible through the generous assistance of the Canada Council for the Arts and the Ontario Arts Council. Book*hug Press also acknowledges the support of the Government of Canada through the Canada Book Fund and the Government of Ontario through the Ontario Book Publishing Tax Credit and the Ontario Book Fund.

Canada Council for the Arts
Conseil des Arts du Canada

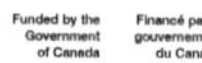

Book*hug Press acknowledges that the land on which we operate is the traditional territory of many nations, including the Mississaugas of the Credit, the Anishnabeg, the Chippewa, the Haudenosaunee, and the Wendat peoples. We recognize the enduring presence of many diverse First Nations, Inuit, and Métis peoples, and are grateful for the opportunity to meet and work on this territory.

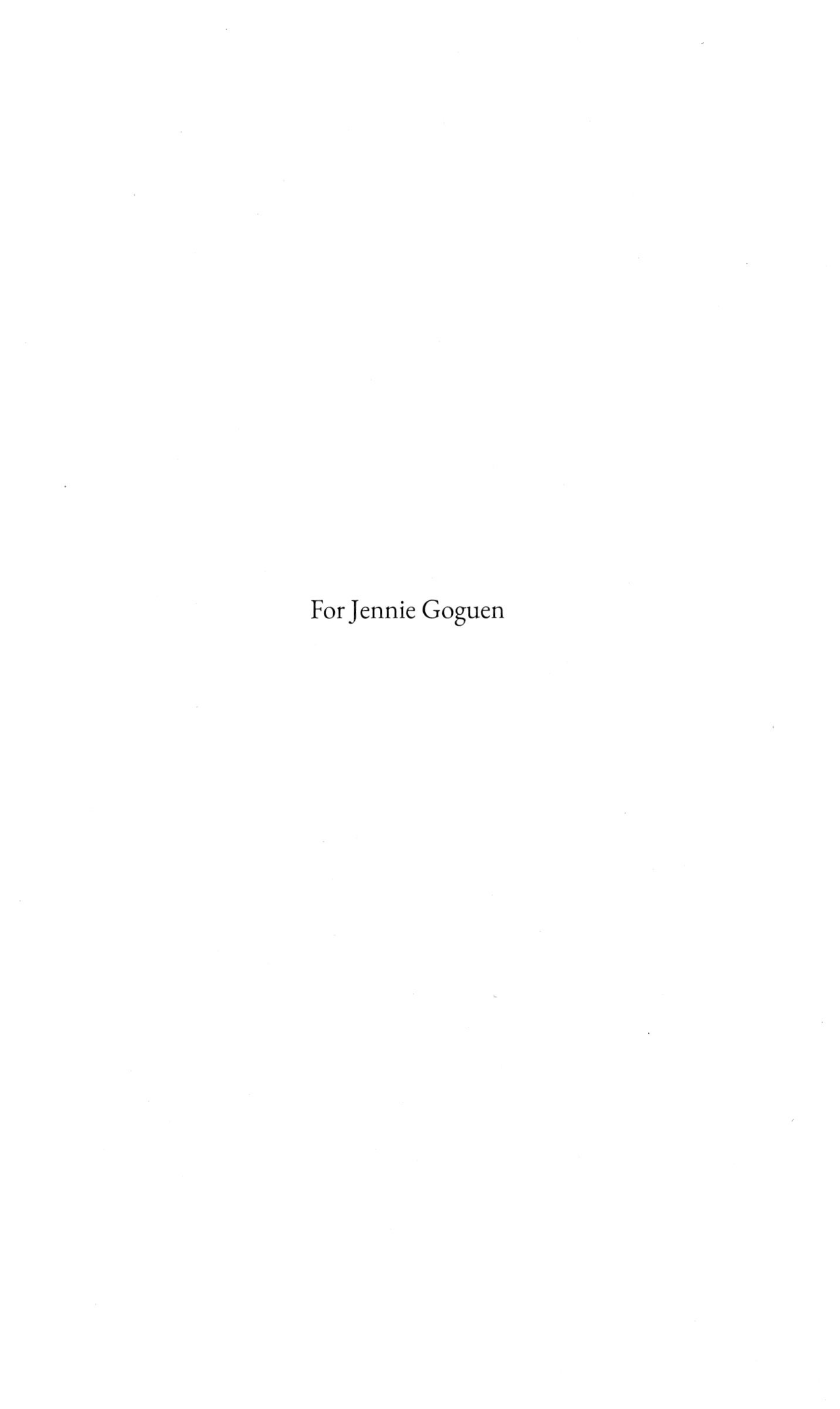

For Jennie Goguen

“Only when access to the imaginative life is denied does one go in for love in a big way”

—VIVIAN GORNICK, *Fierce Attachments*

I wrote a story for you in a journal and it vanished. Yes, vanished. The journal itself disappeared. Where do such missing things go?

In the story I laid down all the things I wanted you to understand. I wanted to write it because, in the years since we lay in the yellow grass, I have come to some knowledge. I cannot recall the contents of the story in full. Because of its loss, I sobbed and felt like the victim of a cruel and unusual fate.

*Do you think you can write it again,* said my mother when I told her.

*In some ways,* I said. *I mean, only in part.*

But the heart of the story is gone and I no longer own it.

Still, my need to speak with you seems to have no end. As I wanted to tell you, in every possible universe, when presented with what you offered me, I take it.

May I begin again?

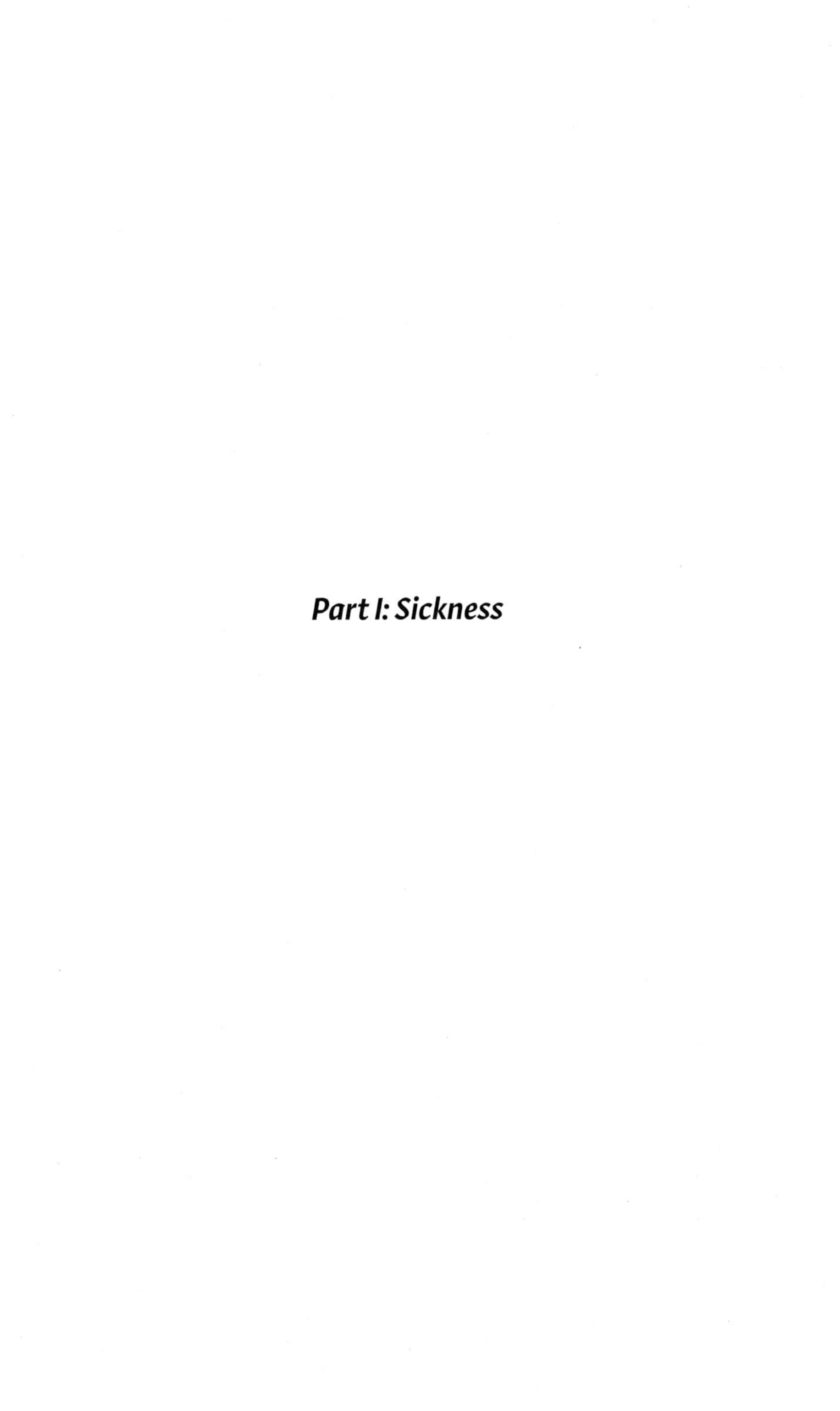

# *Part I: Sickness*

*On My Rights as the Author*

What do you remember of me? Is it difficult to make out? I know your mind, which doesn't take much interest in the past, has possibly let me rot for years. Lacking attention, perhaps the sounds we heard together have shrunk and become difficult to name. The colours you associated with me, mixed together now, present a peculiar new hue. Maybe a bronze, made up of grey lake water and the sun.

Some of my memories of you have been darkened by the things I've heard and seen in the time since we knew one another. Seeing pictures of you online almost removes you more from me; an image of you in red light by the water seems to have nothing to do with you. It is only occasionally that something comes up in front of me—in that hard way virtual things do, so that the rest of the world recedes—and I'm flooded with feeling. For you, I know these memories might have died. For me, they keep. For you, have they simply been discarded? And if they have, to where? What I want to know is, where are the things that have vanished?

For me, very few things end. I can revisit funny memories and put a different name on them. The uncanny ones I've wanted to speak with you about. I am sick to death of being dazzled, of lacking the words. We did not have a love affair.

As I said, I have a story to tell you: a better one than I ever could have come up with at the time I knew you. In many ways, I am teeming with knowledge about what was happening during the time we spent together, and beyond. But I should admit I'm not just trying to pass on the knowledge

I've come to. I also have questions to ask you. Even as I write with vital information I'm bewildered. But the answers I need may be in that place where the vanished objects go, because I am unsure that even you have them.

*On the Beginning*

When I was twelve I lost my mind.

The phrase doesn't bother me. I think it's correct. I lost my mind as accidentally as I lost pencils and five-dollar bills. Maybe my mind flew down the sky to a land of the dead. I don't believe this, of course. But it's better to think it was somewhere.

A gift is frightening. It comes with moorings. I am indebted to you, which makes this whole thing stranger. You overflow, my love. You exceed. For years your gift and its consequences seemed uncontrollable.

Part of you helped me because you wanted to free me. That was the gift you gave. But another part of you wanted to keep me in a contractual relation. Because a gift creates a debtor; gratitude flows forever as all of the gift's effects play out. And in another way you left me so little. I have letters, a T-shirt. There is some documentation of our time together. My unsent emails are a study in bewilderment. When I was twenty I thought about writing to you: *Of course this isn't to overlook the wonderful things you did for me, but I've been thinking about the cost...* Still, however, the uninformed archivist would never be able to sort our data from noise. A colossus of evidence claims we were meaningless to one another. I myself, evaluating it, could make a strong case for barely knowing you.

I could argue the following: there is only one photo of these women together. Neither has ever wished the other merry Christmas. The one card they exchanged said, "Thanks for everything thus far." Therefore, these two women knew each other briefly and then forgot one another. These two women spent a few months together and didn't think much about it after.

But really, the card was written in panic. It implored. "Thus far" actually meant *I must have more*. "Thus far" was intended to mean *I'm old enough now*, although I wrote it when I was very young.

*On Anatomy (I am twelve)*

One is always too young to lose a mind. When I lost mine at age twelve, my universe ruptured. Atypical depression, an underdetermined, mysterious disease of the brain, is strange, and believed by some scientists to be simply a *protest to living*. Feeling cornered, the mind withholds half its sensory and cognitive capacities and leaves the patient with just a little bit of soul to survive on. If I were to write a medical textbook, I would say: The mind shuts off. Intellectual ability devolves, and the acuteness of sensory organs is dramatically reduced. I would explain to students that, when suffering from atypical depression, it becomes very difficult to remember, imagine, and generalize. The afflicted person can only really observe but does not have the sufficient capacity to observe anything fully. There is almost nothing "authentic" remaining. It is a flattening condition, I would tell students, considered to be traumatizing and solitary. I would write with confidence: sadly I became an expert when I got it.

My first psychiatrist was a well-respected researcher. I was very sick when we spoke.

Because of the depression, I couldn't read a book or feel the cold. I existed only when I was witnessed. *Can't you be happy this way?* my psychiatrist asked me. And then he had an art show, a series of acrylic paintings titled *In Sickness and Health*. In his images, patients take on a single form. With the same hands, the same sadness, they need. And then, like a gift, health returns to them. But some of the patients, resisting health, vanish. (I don't know where these patients go, as it is not depicted. They were the subject of only one painting.)

Years ago, when I told you about this art exhibit, I acted like it hadn't affected me. But I will never forget his paintings. They probably shocked me due to his audacity to be good at two things (science and art), when I was not even able to think. I'll spend a life trying to find a word for the feeling of seeing these images. Maybe I will write to you in years when I am old and go, *Yes! That is the word!*

*On Symptomatology (I am twelve–fourteen)*

For your reference: the first symptom was carelessness. I started forgetting my keys every time I left the house. I forgot to zip up my backpack. I forgot homework at school and left my completed assignments at home. I could no longer recall facts as easily. By the time I was thirteen I struggled with internalizing verbal instructions. I couldn't remember my schedule. I forgot forms, gym clothes, library books, money, the day of the week, the way to my doctor's office, and my grandmother's birthday. All around me, others continued to remember.

I stopped paying attention to the weather: it didn't affect me anymore. I tripped constantly. I couldn't play Scrabble. I could no longer balance on skates. By the time I was fourteen, a flatness had set in that was inescapable. By then, I could no longer spell. My favourite novels were just paperweights. My cats were as peripheral as squirrels in the park. Objects, context, lost their ability to affect me. Everything was within reach, but it was no longer received with joy. The boredom was intolerable and so was the horror of losing my emotional connection to art, as the boundary between me and the world widened. I was a quarter of a person, but everyone else stayed whole, continuing to partake in their mysterious consensus about what was happening and what was not.

It might have been better if depression had washed me out of the world, had made it so no one could see me. I might have made an interesting spectator. Instead, throughout my teens I tried to reverse the depressive symptoms through sheer willpower. It did not work, but I tried to bind myself to my flesh, to retrieve all my lost cognitive capacities every day by just trying to process things more clearly. Aware there was suddenly a vacancy in me, I fought against it, at times ruthlessly. I spent hours at the library studying subjects that used to be easy and made myself read long books I couldn't remember or understand anymore. I practised writing constantly, despite the fact that I had lost the ability to generate language properly. I was estranged from whatever it is that is supposed to speak through the writer. Other times I tried to deny that such a thing was even happening. I regulated my thoughts. I began to believe it was possible for a person to deserve to disappear, construing explanations for my cosmic guilt. I concluded that maybe this was simply an ordinary stage of development, that such a shift in consciousness marked the beginning of the entry into adulthood for everybody. It was in this context that heaven seemed to hand me to you.

## *On the History of Uzhhorod*

Trauma wounds a prehistoric part of the brain, which predates the human capacity for speech. Therefore language fails to describe trauma. Being beyond language is trauma's inherent trait. A number of scientists have written about this.

What triggered this depression? It might have been predetermined. The reptilian mind carries a history, and mine was predisposed for this kind of thing, if the epigenetic theory that trauma intrudes on our genes is true. It's not known why, but women manifest Jewish trauma more keenly than men. My father's father went through the war and had only one son, meaning I was the first woman who descended from the Jews of Uzhhorod, Czechoslovakia, in my family. Maybe that had a hand in it. When I got sick, the doctors reeled. *What happened?* they asked me when my body displayed the signs of significant trauma. *What happened to you?* I couldn't say. I didn't know.

I've looked into the history a little more recently. In 1944, 99.9 per cent of the Jews of Uzhhorod vanished. Some worked as forced labour for companies. But then they disappeared too. The history was documented only by those who didn't know it in its entirety, who found false identification or were shipped to labour battalions in the east.

But their sorrow festers. Maybe it flared up in me. Or it didn't and it lives elsewhere, sitting with the other disappeared and stolen things.

*On Epiphany (I am twelve–fourteen)*

It might not have been an outrageous fate set out for me before I had time to become a teenager. Why else would a twelve-year-old brain shut off? My other guess is that maybe I was overwhelmed with frightening knowledge before I was ready. (Do I have your attention? I have for so long wished to lay this out for you.) This anxiety, of course, you know about; it was the initial reason for our conversations. When I was twelve, a realization overthrew me. Suddenly I couldn't look at photographs of myself as a child. The content of dreams, once mysterious, began to frighten me. Feeling infected, I related much less to my mother and filled up my diaries with lies. My language, reddened by terror, was split a few degrees from the truth. I now spoke a dialect with a fresh influence, a distinct etymology. It denied, to both listener and speaker.

Twelve was too young to be queer, but in the world we've made one is always a little too young for the knowledge, could always have had another few years or months. I anticipated the necessity of running away, following ostracization. My unlived future, like an echo, diminished and died.

*On Middle School (I am twelve–fourteen)*

The year I turned twelve, men came—in shadowy clothes faded in memory—to deliver me into my sickness. They were teachers, my doctor. *What is wrong with you?* Unwilling to live in a world where I had gone mad, to consider the possibility that I had symptoms of a disease that was practically impossible to treat, my family and I chose to inhabit a world in which, by one standard, I was wicked. My father was a refugee, and the logic of immigration is that the new place is safe. Anything bad that happens in the new place originates from within. The problem that afflicted me, therefore, had to be of my own making. Wickedness to many of the people around me was *not doing one's best*, losing everything, feeling nothing, *wasting*, as they say, like a broken machine. Idleness was evil, and work that led to self-sufficiency, no matter its consequences, was good because it demonstrated work ethic, the highest, most perfect ideal. Any problem can be overcome this way, and no problem can be bigger than what the family has already faced. Best of all, a strong work ethic breeds knowledge, the one thing that under no circumstances can be taken away.

In this vision of good and evil, every event has been inflicted on the self. From this perspective, disability is impossible.

## *On the Significance of Names*

Even when I finally got a name for the disease (*atypical depression*), I still suspected it was not solely psychiatric. It felt demonic. I lived in a room above my own head because something had stolen my body. There are so many worlds; I might have passed through too many. Every stage of mental illness was so different that I worry we are unintelligible to one another. In the end, the only thing I felt I had the power to do while I was depressed was name things. I chose names for different concepts. This is misery. This is beauty. And this, I thought when I was eighteen and had you as a counsellor, is finding a double. This is companionship. I suppose that was around the time I began to map you onto everything I saw.

After I met you I told you my secret and then you began to tell me yours. The seams of my universe parted. When we met, I imagined your world with a white horizon; I thought it was changeless, with identical nights.

## *On the Number Twenty-Seven*

The knowledge I want to communicate to you, the questions I need to ask, are partly a defence. I want to prove to you that I'm not ridiculous.

The matter is a little pressed for time. When we met, I'd been eighteen for two weeks. Your age at the time has held significance to me for years. I believed when I turned twenty-seven I would understand.

You see, I'm now twenty-six. I've only just recovered from the long depression. I haven't seen you in seven years; I won't again. I need to write our story down while I'm as close as I'll ever be to you as you were when we knew one another. At this moment I can sort old impressions into categories. I can see which of your traits were simply the product of being twenty-seven and which were really representative of you. Soon I'll age away from you as you are in my memory. I'm afraid of being too easy on you once you seem young.

*Do you want to talk tonight?* you used to ask me.

Sickness's companion is shame. When I was depressed, my teachers told me I was bad, reckless, lazy, silly, and thankless.

Your gift-giving, the favour you did me, created a debt, but it still met a need: it offset all the derision. I find myself fearing the shape of my life if I hadn't met you. You may be different now, but when I knew you, you were all force, emitting terror and joy all at once. Your motion was continuous.

Can you fathom how starved I was when we met? I was eighteen, and because of the depression I had not felt the heat in six years. I couldn't imagine, nor could a painting move me. Like a sun, you fed light into me. I was careless at that time. I risked losing myself to you on a whim.

*On My Intentions*

I will describe how we met and how I fell in love with you. I turned eighteen two weeks before we met. I had been in the closet and missing my mind for six years. Due to the depression, my intellectual capacity had plummeted and my senses were severely dulled. I knew something within me had been lost and I found this terrifying but did not know what the problem was. I did know, however, that I needed to figure out how to be queer in the world. Seeking transformation at any cost, I resolved to come out before I started university. Whatever part of me was left behind while I was depressed was focused and detective-like. It overturned problems meticulously and executed each possible solution with the seriousness of self-preservation. The only reason I met with you in the first place, the only thing I ever let on I needed your help with, was to come out.

If mental illness was the first rupture of my universe, you were the second. I'll present the evidence I have to prove this. But you have to read this story to the end. You see, there was a third rupture, after you.

*On "Coming Out" (I am eighteen)*

Last June in Toronto, the prime minister waved a flag with every colour. People like us are now encouraged to come out. We are told it was all a misunderstanding, and there is nothing the matter with us. We are encouraged to forget the past in which we were perverse. But it is always different with mothers.

Your mother told you you'd go to hell. I was petrified to come out to mine. And people like us feel removed from our mothers, who cannot raise us in our new world. So we look for instruction. The archives contain very little; there aren't any monuments for us. But a mother condemning a daughter to hell is an unrecorded event: there are no statistics on the matter. It must happen every moment, because I believe it was always happening to you once it occurred.

For me, coming out was like backing away, like letting the old world recede. I felt displaced and I turned to you violently. Can you blame me for it?

Toronto is considered a nice place for people like us; at the time, you could not even get married in your state. You thought it would be a good city to work in while you were waiting to start a job in California in November, and you signed a three-month contract to fill in for a therapist who went on leave. Over July, August, and September of the summer I was eighteen, I walked into your office on Mondays for Mentorship, a counselling service associated with the university I had deferred acceptance to for a year. *You'll be with Iris,* they told me. So you were assigned as my counsellor. I looked to the left, and you were walking down the hallway in a red T-shirt with your hair tied up. You stood in front of a window.

*On the Coffee Shop by the Office (I am eighteen)*

This was how you became my guide to the margins of things. When we met, I could tell it was easy for you to introduce yourself to new people and I assumed you wouldn't like me that much. But I was surprised by how *kindly* you looked at me when I blurted out what I needed help with. I was surprised that you thought I was funny. You asked me little questions, had me recount when I knew, how it felt. You had perfected the habits of listening. And then one afternoon you said quietly, *You're exactly like I was when I was coming out.* I had never really met anyone queer before. It had felt like something I would never share with anybody. The subway broke down a few stations from my house that afternoon, and I walked home through the Humber ravine feeling completely exhilarated.

You were so keen to tell me what to do next. Worried I needed more help with coming out, you offered to meet three times a week until I told my friends. *You know what, we could talk at the coffee shop by the office on Wednesdays and Fridays too,* you said. They were doing construction at the office and the paint-primer smell spread out through the room. It felt natural we would want to talk somewhere quieter that didn't smell like chemicals. It felt easy to say, *Yes, we should.* I was so young that, the first time we met there, I didn't even know how to order a coffee.

*Dark or medium roast?*

*What?* I said.

As days and then weeks passed, you began to make promises. You told me terrible things wouldn't happen. You told me no one would mind. Everything, you promised me, would hold.

Things had a shape. Things somehow organize themselves. *After all, we just happened to meet when you needed help with this,* you said while you stretched your arm over your chair. Your palm was facing the floor. There was something careless about it.

You always spoke about the structure of the universe with confidence. We accelerate into the future, you told me. One day we flare up fully formed. *This is how you do it.* You promised. *Tell them.* I confessed more to you each time we met. And I thought: *What a fluke we were put together. I am so lucky to know her.*

You taught me by your movements. I had the feeling that in the fold of your hand was a picture of the world.

*On Wanting*

You always wanted to be a mother. Eight years have passed, and I don't think you are one. I remember you would sigh and say, *I'd like a family soon,* as if I was old enough to weigh in on whether or not you should have children. I could tell you were surrounded by desires I didn't yet understand. When you said it the first time, I felt far away from you. But women like us are never really seen as mothers; the ordinary things the world commands us to need, promises us are within us, are still somehow withheld from us. Is that why we're lonely?

The picture of yourself you gave to me when we met slackened and started to give as the months passed. Your essence, the object of this search, began to seep through. I saw it everywhere but couldn't take it.

*On Gossip (I am eighteen)*

I declared my feelings about you gracelessly, in everything I did. We must have looked ridiculous together. Our sessions constantly went overtime, and we often lingered in the hallway talking while someone else waited to speak with you. The first time this happened, you kept a hand on your doorway as if you were about to go back into your office. I took my sunglasses out of my bag and held them like I was about to leave. But we kept talking, contradicting the image we made of two people about to part. So much force drove the conversations.

Your colleagues sensed something unusual was happening. *You're supposed to have ten-minute breaks in between—you can't go past the hour,* one of them reminded you, suddenly very concerned with the office schedule. And people I knew encouraged me, with almost primal compulsion, to stop seeing you. It was like they needed to keep the world in its natural form, to prevent the occurrence of something very unexpected. Through no intentional coordination, my friends and family moved to discourage us from meeting so frequently. *What could you possibly have in common with her?* my friend asked me when I paused telling a story. I crossed my arms and catalogued the incident as evidence I was right that something strange was playing out.

But truthfully, though people whispered, gave advice, hinted in language and gesture, what was happening between us was never taken too seriously: it seemed to be understood as fundamentally unprofound. I don't think a man and a woman in that office would have gotten away with it. I could tell our behaviour was perceived as weird, as annoying, but not as destructive.

Whenever I left the office through the courtyard, the winds rose. I felt I knew too much.

*On Cheating on an Ex (I am eighteen)*

It seemed to me that the substance that formed between us while we spoke in the office and at the coffee shop was immaterial, or at least a pure force. I thought it was energy, proof of the overflow of your soul. Now I think it might have been daylight. Daylight as substance. Daylight as what everything craves.

Beneath everything, something in you seemed molten. As the weeks passed, like the plates of the earth, you couldn't hold. Gaps formed. Thoughts escaped. You were heartbroken and had destroyed something recently. For a moment on the patio outside the café, over our coffees in July, your face expressed your spirit so clearly. Your eyebrows contracted like someone had touched them.

*I left our place in Colorado really quickly, I barely thought it through,* you said. *I went straight to my parents' house in California.*

*I chose to cheat on her,* you told me. Behind you, the arm of the tower crane by your office rose.

You were always in combat with reluctance, but you started to tell me things about yourself; in the café, with only strangers to bear witness, our sessions departed from the topic of me coming out. We started to muse about life or you'd ask me questions about beauty or love. I thought over what it was you wanted to hear and repeated it back to you. Each time you admitted something to me about yourself, I was astonished. There was nothing like it. You first hinted and then started to say you were bad, that you felt there was wickedness in you.

Maybe you don't remember. But you sometimes said you'd housed it since you were a girl. It could be true. Everything happens, even unspeakable things.

*I need to figure out how to take responsibility for it,* you said on one of the first days you talked to me about cheating on your last girlfriend, Eva. I wondered if you thought I knew a secret. I watched bewilderment run across your face, and the pop song playing in the coffee shop reached a crescendo.

*On the Origin of Our Universe (I am eighteen)*

Today I am young. Yes, I am young. And I am the age you were when we met. But when I met you at eighteen, wisdom seemed to course through you. In our conversations you sifted through leagues of memories, justified claims with your fore-knowledge: *I know, but you'll see.* So many things you said I would see. You fed your fingertips through your hair. Every Monday your office exuded protectiveness, authority—the signs were your hand pressing into the wall, the sealike lake outside the window, the sun always visible in our afternoons. I would not be injured here, everything testified. I would be *uninjured.*

I would never have loved you if we'd met on equal footing. I think you know this. I think you know that you've done wrong, *took from me* while you oversaw me. These kinds of matters come to theft: a carrying over from one woman to another. Wherever you are, drinking in forgetfulness, *things do not simply end*. As I write to you, if you've read this far, these things happened and you must think of them.

On the day of our sixth meeting, I came to you very quickly. It was the third time we met at the coffee shop. While we sat in the corner, I watched light in the window pass over the asphalt and I told you I couldn't stop thinking about a memory from childhood. You spoke to me in a tone of jealousy suddenly, said you didn't think about things enough after they happened. *You feel things so many times, don't you,* you said a little offhandedly. It was the first time in my life I had ever felt like I was seeing straight through someone. A circle of stillness formed. As a world was made from nothing, the air denied that it used to move. In a wave of grief, I started to love you. It seemed to take up a *vacant space* in me, the space I later realized was left empty when depression took away my ability to imagine. It was a *mitzvah*, a miracle on earth. As we all have done, I kept silent about what had happened. Taking note from the histories of women like us, I did not even write down that I had fallen in love with you.

*On a Paradigm*

When I started loving you I learned love subsumed vanity, even shame. The embarrassment of the situation ebbed in the periphery, but my god, I flowed with you. A contraction of your lips, and I vanished. I saw everything twice, by me and by you—you were *always in front of me.* I can't capture it. In memory even, I fear it.

*On Eva (I am eighteen)*

We spoke on a bus. We had met at the coffee shop late that day and talked for nearly four hours. When we got to your stop, you said, *Let's keep talking.*

*Why are you wearing all of that makeup,* you said.

*I don't know. Why do you care.*

*Your eyes are lovely.*

You had rules for living well, most of them arbitrary.

*My mom is not impressed with me,* you said. *She's mad I'm still taking these fake counselling jobs. She thinks I should get a master's or something.*

*You'd be good at that.*

*She wants me to start a practice, maybe.*

*Did she like Eva?*

*No. She thought she was too quiet. She didn't understand why I liked her.*

*She would hate me then,* I said.

*No, of course not. Is it crossing lines talking about this?*

*No!*

*Okay. Yeah, she hated her,* you said. *I wish I could tell Eva I loved her. I don't think she believes that I did, but I did.*

*I feel like she knows.*

*She definitely doesn't. I want to call her but I think it's just because I'm afraid to be lonely again. Anyway, you look so concerned. What are you thinking about?*

*I'm afraid.*

We sat very close. The bus passed my stop. We spoke until it was midnight. You took your hand and traced my face like you were skimming water. A man and a woman came onto the bus together, and you moved your hand away very quickly. The woman looked over. I felt ridiculous, and consumed.

*On Jealousy, and the Content of Souls (I am eighteen)*

Today, at twenty-six, I am fascinated by people I meet who were like me as children: who were curious and wanted to be writers one day. I peer at them as if across an inlet of water: *What are your sorrows?* I ask my doubles. If only we could live out every life, but sickness culls possible worlds, lets everything spoil.

When I met other people similar to me in university, people who wanted to be writers but had never lost their minds, they seemed to think their luck was the work of providence. To them, their souls had not been snatched, and so they did not believe anything like this was possible. Sometimes, until something is taken it does not exist. I suppose I am jealous. But I'm still surprised by my anger at others for having what I used to think wasn't possible to lose.

When I met you I saw you as a kind of double of mine, a double who took a path I did, like we'd both been infected by something sinister while we were young. Your language always held a second meaning, always concealed, but you did say, *Maybe I think you're myself.* While you said it, you looked just over my head at the pendulum clock they had in the coffee shop. I wondered if you needed to leave. But we stayed for another hour. Being similar women of different ages, we maybe found it too hard to pass up the chance to speak across time. Up until that moment, I had always been with people my own age, something that made me feel like only the present existed. But you backed into me and I reeled. I leaned into a terrible possible future. *Let me grow to be unlike her,* I wrote, even as I sought to live out a life with you, in different forms, for years.

A diary is no longer a diary once it is read. When you showed me an old one of yours, a password-protected online blog, it frightened me. When *you* were eighteen you sensed within yourself a destructive talent. You were charming, and so you had many more possibilities than other people; you chose between dozens of lives. "Why do I wreck everything I have?" you wrote. At the time I knew you, your touch counted as ten ordinary ones. I felt you rearrange mass, unform entities. Systems of force, closed for millennia, seemed to split open for you.

But was it the world you ruled, or simply me?

*On the Art of Rhetoric (I am eighteen)*

I was always writing in a notebook at that time. I thought I could order things. I thought things could be made to make sense.

*One of my old students let me read her journals,* you said. *They were really boring. I found it so sweet.*

*I would be so embarrassed to show someone mine.*

*Why?* you asked, like I'd said something peculiar.

*I don't know, it's humiliating.*

*Why?*

*What do you mean by "Why?"*

*I mean, why would it be shameful to show.*

At some point I must have agreed to let you read it. What did you say to convince me? I can't remember. All I have is the journal itself, which takes on a ridiculous style midway through. It's the thing I crafted for you. It's the way I made myself seem so you'd love me back. *What was I really thinking half the time?* I don't know. All I know is what you read. At the time, you hated evasion and wanted everyone to express themselves exactly as they were. You wanted the diary to reproduce my mind and seemed to believe this was possible.

In the café you would say, *Can I read what you've been writing?* and stretch your hand out before I said yes, like a diary was an ordinary thing for one woman to give to another. So I'd show you the next part of the journal. Your grip on my wrist tightened and loosened according to the flow of certain passages. You adored it.

I would never be so creative again. I wrote down what I

thought you would love. I pressed all my best guesses at who I would have been if I hadn't lost my mind into a single person for you and held it together like if I let go I was going to die.

After you left the city, it was difficult to look at the journal. I'd open it and think, *This is the thing she wanted to read?* Every page is evasive. I wrote a lot about coming out, but I never wrote about the feeling that you had replaced an inexplicable emptiness in me. While writing these diary entries for you, I tried to deny the feeling I had had for years that I seemed to have lost my mind. Every entry anticipates my fear that you will figure out that something is missing from me. Every entry says, *I am a soul, please don't look any deeper.* The process reminded me of writing diary entries about boys I was trying to convince myself I had a crush on when I was in middle school.

There is a difference between the diary I wrote for you and the few notes I wrote for myself on sheets of paper I kept in my bedroom. In the diary entries you read, I write about you like you're an object of intellectual curiosity. I am parsing through you, politely and meticulously. I am passionate about you as a scientific object. In the two brief passages I wrote in my room that I knew no one would ever see, I am fanatical with interest in you.

Do you see? There is nothing honest to archive! There is no proper account. I have memories, a few emails, and nothing more besides these short notes I jotted down when I was alone. Even the online blog you shared with me was taken down by the server.

*On Favourites (I am eighteen)*

On one night toward the end of August, we spoke with our coffees on a park bench. I was holding my knees.

You said, *You must trust me a lot.*

*I do,* I said.

*It feels nice to be trusted again. I can honestly be such a bad person. I mean it this time. Well, I've done more bad things than I've told you about. Sorry if I'm being too open. I think I'm really tired.*

*But you helped me so much.*

*Yeah, but I'm so shit at my job right now.*

*I don't think so.*

But you had begun to neglect the other students you were supposed to be counselling. Our sessions went overtime.

*I barely listened to her,* you would say about the girl whose appointment was before mine. *You're more interesting. What have you been thinking about?* Or you would cancel on them last-minute.

*I know you're having a hard week, but I feel like shit today,* you texted me. *Could you just come to my apartment tonight? Would you bring your journal? I want to read as much of your writing as I can.*

The place where you lived on College Street was above a hair salon that played elevator music all day. None of the black furniture was yours; the only out-of-place item was a hammock hanging between two posts in the living room. You had packed in a hurry. All you really brought with you from California was your clothes, mostly bright-coloured T-shirts you collected and discarded as you moved from city to city.

On your balcony, the clouds threw dark shadows. You asked me how I was feeling and told me I should come out to my friends next week. You made me promises that you'd be different once you were home in California.

*Does our age difference bother you? I mean, we can be friends, right?*

*No, I don't care,* I said. *Of course we can.*

*You're the only person in my life who isn't annoying me right now.*

You believed everything should be confessed. You believed you had a claim on all of me.

To you, nothing was as terrible as a secret.

Did you know that the mind can have a single thought? Blending my form with yours to give you everything you wanted, I waited for you to explain what it was you were doing to me.

*On Mining the Universe (I am eighteen)*

I came out to my friends. It had seemed completely impossible before I met you, and it remains the most counterintuitive thing I have ever done. My friend said, *How do you know?* and I almost physically flinched in discomfort. I stared longingly at my phone, wanting to text you. Nobody ditched me, but the awkwardness I felt with them afterwards made me long for you even more. I felt my old world closing behind me, and everything fixing onto you. It all seemed prior to you, as if the city and its inhabitants would not exist for much longer anyway and it made sense to spend our time together.

The day after I came out to my friends it was your twenty-seventh birthday. I thought mournfully that I had no reason to speak with you at the café anymore. The whole explanation for meeting outside of your office was that I needed help coming out. And now I had descended into a life world in which only you existed, in which my feelings for you filled up the gap in me that depression had created. I rushed to the bookstore that day to buy you a birthday present and got you a book about a man who ferries passengers across a lake. The writer talked about the water like it was an animal.

The card I wrote for you said, *Dear Iris, happy birthday. Thanks for everything thus far.* I think the purpose of the card was to draw you into my future, to promise you that my need exceeded what you had given me. Later that afternoon my friends and I went to Centre Island. I spent the whole time looking at the long shadows cast by the clouds, collecting stories and visions for you.

In my memory, September and October seem to have happened in a different country. Having come out practically to impress you, I thought our time speaking so frequently would finish. But it didn't. In those strange months, you spun your canvas of lawlessness.

*On Conspiracy (I am eighteen)*

*Should we meet at the café at six?*

*Sure sounds good. You* asked *me*. Posing as friends, time seeming to gather speed, we continued to meet at the coffee shop like it was what we'd planned all along. *How did it go telling your friends?* you asked me, full of concern. But we moved on to different topics within fifteen minutes or so. This time *I* anxiously watched the copper pendulum in the café swing and hoped we would stay sitting there for longer. We did. When I got home I barely reacted to being locked out of my parents' house. I sank onto the doorstep. I looked at the street, and gradually my gaze settled on the sky.

You and I had so many incentives to mean nothing to each other. It was embarrassing running off together in front of your co-workers, and I always got weird looks when I said I was leaving home to see you. But we just kept doing it. Whatever was driving us to meet was an internal compulsion related only to our perception of one another.

The other participant in our life together was Fortune. I ran into you over and over again in the city, and you would laugh and say, *Of course you just turned up here.* This is why I felt handed over to you sometimes, by something beyond my will.

You were only here for three months. You would leave in October. Did this deadline give us the excuse to rush things? There was never, never time. We often said we were trying to cover as many topics as we could before you had to leave. Do you remember the theatre of it? We began to play out excuses for meeting more often, sometimes at your apartment. *Well, we don't have that long anyway,* you would say. *You might as well just come by.*

In our evening conversations, your soul emerged in fragments that receded if I looked directly at them. While we talked, you slipped in and out of a self-righteous tone, caught me in a mess of dialects in which you spoke like a counsellor, spoke like a friend, and drew your fingers slowly through my hair. At that point, I had never been so attracted to someone in my life. I used to literally swoon; my breath caught in my throat, time to time, and I had to look down in the middle of speaking. Your smell ran through me again and again.

Over time I began to treat the world beyond you as merely a resource from which to gather the content of our discussions. This habit, once acquired, is very difficult to break.

*On the Only Ideal That Can Be Grasped Through Sensation*

Your body was all angles; your face was sculpted to draw attention to the eyes. When I looked at them I would think of Anne Carson's collection *The Beauty of the Husband,* where she writes about John Keats and his theory of beauty. I would think, *He was right: beauty is truth, the only perfection on earth.* Nothing else has ever prompted me to think, *He was right!* in that way again. I was obsessed with the image of you. I was obsessed with your arms and your expressions. I don't understand why I haven't thought anything else was more perfect. Why not a mountain? Why not a more beautiful woman I dated? I have never wanted someone to touch me so much.

*On Unity (I am eighteen)*

On the first day of September I came to your apartment and talked with your roommate Stephen before you got home. He had silver-blue eyes.

*What do you want to study?* he asked me.

*I'm not sure yet.*

*You like writing, right?*

*Yeah.*

*That's cool, you can do a lot with that.*

*What do you work in?*

*I'm in film.* He paused. *So you're really close with Iris?* he said.

I realized he thought the whole thing was a bit funny. You came home, and I automatically started walking to your room. When I shut the door he was watching us from down the hallway.

*Where do you want to talk?*

*I don't know,* I said.

*Then here?*

*Sure.*

For the first time we lay in your bed. I was never the same because afterwards I remembered it.

*I'm just feeling guilty again,* you said.

*About what?*

*Can I tell you another day?*

*Definitely.*

*What are you thinking about?*

*I don't know,* I said. *I was thinking about trying to thank you.*

*Oh well, that's fine, you don't need to do that.*

You hated compliments. They were the only things that made you awkward. You didn't believe them.

*Your last journal entry made me speechless,* you said. *It made me cry.*

*The one about wanting to be one person?*

*Yeah,* you said.

*I feel like so many,* I said.

*Me too, it's like I'm different in every room.*

*I feel like I need to organize you into categories,* I said. You laughed, but I was being completely serious.

*Did I ask you too much what you were thinking today?* you asked me. *I don't know why I care so much. I just wanted to get out of my head.*

*I don't mind,* I said. I couldn't mind. I wanted to give you it all.

For a while your capacity to listen to me seemed impossibly generous, especially in the beginning. But I think you were right when you said that you wanted to get out of your head. I think that to you your own mind was violent, so you sought out mine.

When we kissed the first time there, on the bed, it seemed not to have happened immediately afterwards. You became cold, and you told me you were getting tired. The voice you used to speak with me was the same one you used when you had talked to me the first few times we met in your office.

It was probably the best moment of my life. I went home feeling like I was going to throw up. I would have left the city with you. All I thought about was how to make it happen again.

*We should meet at the beach to talk, this week,* you texted me, after saying nothing for a day. I lay in my bed and wondered and wanted you.

*On What the Sea Gave (I am eighteen)*

It was cold by the water. Wind rolled through waves. Men and women walked by and we'd move apart.

*Why do I like talking to you so much?* you said. *Do I think you're myself?*

You said, *Stephen said I should talk to you less. He said it's a bit weird. I mean, I think it's fine. I can have a friend.*

*Of course.*

*He acts like he's my friend but he's not* really *my friend. And my co-workers are boring. I burned a lot of bridges in Colorado and it's so nice to have someone I'm close with.*

*I'm not as afraid to tell my parents,* I said. *I think it's going to be okay.*

You looked like I'd harmed you. *I'm so happy for you,* you said.

I had seen you look at me in the same way before. It was envy, I think. You were quiet.

You said, *I have to stop wrecking everything that I touch.*

You said, *We should go camping after I leave. Or something.*

*I think so too.*

We lay in the sand. While you touched my face and my hair, you said, *I don't even really know what I need. Do you want to talk tomorrow night too?*

Yes. My god.

The sky was so low and so grey. Nothing fit anymore. Things had lost their edges and their shape was only clear after they had vanished.

There was trash on the beach. The lake spit up driftwood

and egg cartons, as if to say, *This is the rot of it; this is the proof. Other things have happened.*

I remember the heat of your breath while you spoke. The only sound other than you was what the waves let out. The water seemed full. It had had so much time.

*On Getting Blessings (I am eighteen)*

*It is so bizarre that we met,* you would say. *It's just so strange. This is exactly what I would have wanted to help someone with.*

You had taken the job last-minute and dropped into the city on a whim, lacking any history or context. You didn't know anybody here. The counselling service initially put me with somebody else. *She took a leave of absence,* you said. *So then they put us together. It's just such a fluke that you needed help with this.* Even your mother in an email said it was "fateful" that we had met.

Currents of motion beyond our control created perfect conditions. We always bumped into each other.

*Why does this happen?* you asked me after we ran into each other at the drugstore. You were wearing a green shirt that said the name of a summer camp in Maine. The backlight from the makeup stand lit up your edges. *Have you wondered why this always happens?* You stood in the middle of the aisle, and a man around my age had to lean into the shelves of hair dye to get past you. He diminished in the periphery until he no longer existed.

I thought, *The world loved me until it didn't and then it did again.*

So it seemed, for a while, that nature did everything. This shameful thing, this love, had been sanctioned by something divine.

As the weeks passed I began to hope that we could be timeless. I began to hope that, like Plato's myth of creation, we could have been split in the early days of history and when we found each other just clung at one another. Until we did nothing. Until we folded in an embrace, every law determined by Desire, the eldest of the gods.

I still couldn't feel the cold; I spoke from madness, the densest place in the world. But with you, light seemed to lift off the water outside the window of your office. The dark, before impossibly low, rose.

During that September, you seemed to believe that I owed you all of my thoughts. Every evening you whispered your language of misery. Only your compliments fed me. *Your eyes, today,* you would say. Or, *No one I've met has ever made me think so much!* Any disappointment I caused you led to crisis. If I seemed reticent, you were instantly cold. And the compulsion to speak with you was like an order, a country of wanting I thought I would live in forever. Drawn like everyone to the water, we met there again, then again, almost nightly. I had never been to these lakeside bluffs before I knew you: you found them as substitutes for the nature you missed in California. Plains of water in purples and greens made it seem like we weren't in a city with rules.

We probably kissed four or five times, in total. And every time it happened, the next day you would call me your friend or even your student, which restored our official relationship so effectively that the situation felt briefly hopeless. I was so hungry for you I felt sick. We never slept together. The only place on me you ever touched was my back.

*On Playing God (I am eighteen)*

I was so in love that I practically forgot how unwell I felt. Telling you I had the feeling something had vanished from me years before never occurred to me; I was too afraid of you to even consider making a confession like that. Instead I hid my fears about the depression from you exactingly and in the process tried to continue to conceal it from myself. I denied that I couldn't follow the plot of a movie. I denied that I seemed not to be able to imagine. It was simply not part of the universe I wanted to make for us. I didn't want us to know that something like this was even possible.

*On Transgressions (I am eighteen)*

One day, I walked in on you sobbing in your bedroom.

*I slept with a friend's ex in June,* you said to me. *I don't know, it's probably fine. I was just so alone at the time.*

*We're both going to be okay,* I said.

Your hand covered your eyes.

*Someone I know does tarot readings,* you said. *I don't believe in them but he told me there were seven women behind me that I've hurt. I can't stop thinking about it. I need to be better, but I've always said that.*

Sun passed over the oil paintings of trees on the wall of your living room. I wished the apartment wasn't a sublet and that you had picked the artwork so it would mean something about you. There were pictures of tourist sites in France and Italy framed by the dresser in your bedroom, but there were no photographs of people. Even the photo of Pisa depicted the tower on an empty lawn without any tourists.

*I'm afraid of hell,* you said. *I can't get it out of my head.*

At the time, I thought I was bad too. I was terrified of becoming you.

Sometimes you ignored me for days without explanation or purpose. Then you'd text me, *We should talk tonight,* and the earth reclaimed its axis, spun on its wheel again. We made lists of things to discuss. They breached forty, fifty topics and contained subjects we had no knowledge of. We tried to hold the world by its hands and apportion it. We looked on to the heavens and tried to utter them. Every night we spoke quickly, as if a minute could be lengthened. Our whispers thickened the air and settled into your sheets. The most intimate nights we didn't kiss. You forgot to pretend we were friends, and your stare was so unselfconscious it felt violating.

Do you remember how much you wanted to know of me? Do you remember that *you set a timer and asked me what I was thinking every fifteen minutes?*

*On Contradiction (I am eighteen)*

There was a single time I said no to you. At your apartment in your living room I wrote, *I'm in love?* in my journal, desperate to tell something. We were sitting on your couch.

*Can I read what you're writing?* you asked very suddenly.

After I said you couldn't, you walked to the other side of the room. By the painting of the sycamore tree, you looked out the window. I left in misery.

*Why did you leave?* you texted me while I was walking to the subway. *I was waiting for you to come talk to me.*

Wind upset the ends of the trees, tossing them into the sun. I wanted to stop it. I wanted to close the jaws of the sky, which yawned like they were going to let in the dead. I felt so afraid you might have started to suspect—as I did—that something was very wrong with me. My feelings for you, my dependency on you, petrified me. But there was nothing to do; tenderness for you ran through me at every moment. The depression had taken everything from me at that point, besides the violent capacity I had to love you. I blacked out the sentence in pen, turned around, and went back to you.

*What would I have done without you,* I said.

*You would have been fine,* you said.

*Hopefully. It was just impossible to come out before I met you. I didn't have any images. I didn't know what I was supposed to do.*

*You would have been fine.*

To this day I don't know if I would have been. I was so sick. I needed you. I wish I had a better record of what happened between us. Looking over the diary now, I blacked out other passages I thought would hurt you. I am desperate to know what they say. But if I hadn't been writing it for you, I don't think we would have ever gotten as close as we did. At times I wrote my feelings in code. I wrote little comments in French, which you didn't speak, or I signified your name with an *X*. I wrote in the margins, *I am losing my mind. I am terrorized and so happy.*

One afternoon we were talking in your office while you played with my hair. Your colleague knocked and opened the door. I jumped and my knees bumped into the top of the table in front of me, but you looked completely unaffected and took your hand away from my face. After she left, you continued speaking to me like nothing had happened.

*On the Train (I am eighteen)*

*Is it hard holding hands?* I asked you one night on your couch. You were lying on your back in the hammock and your feet were touching my leg.

*It's fine. You get a few weird looks. Sometimes you get compliments.*

*I'm scared about making people uncomfortable.*

*You're way braver than me,* you said. *You'll be fine.*

*Would you date a man?*

Suddenly you looked very young. Quietly you said, *It would be easier.*

We returned to things you had told me right when we met.

*A man yelled at me at a train station after I kissed Eva goodbye,* you said.

*Yeah, you told me that.* But you had told me that like it was funny.

*It was terrible. He kept saying, "You can't do that here."*

*I'm overwhelmed. Weren't you overwhelmed?*

*I mean, I remember thinking, "Shit, I'm going to have to be rich to have kids."*

*That's it?*

*I don't know,* you said. Quietly you said my name. *I'm different. I can't feel things all the time. I would die.*

*On Absence (I am eighteen)*

Light at the horizon broadened and vanished while I walked to you. Night fell all over me.

I was quiet at your apartment.

You said, *What's wrong?*

*Nothing. How are you?*

*Should you be seeing your friends?*

*I could,* I said.

*I just worry.*

Nothing else seemed to be happening. I was neglecting my friends and would always leave them if you texted me that you wanted to speak. My friends looked at me like they didn't understand me, and since I'd come out I didn't feel like I could hug anybody. It drew me into you even more. I needed to peel everything back; I needed *clarity.* I waited for you to tell me you were in love with me, for sex, for anything. Time rushed forward. We had four weeks until you would leave the city. The more I longed to understand you, the more my fear you might understand me seemed to grow.

You said, *God, I* missed *you all day.*

I wondered what was beneath your expressions that would sort everything into order. I worried I would never get past what I saw. What if there wasn't anything underneath it at all?

*On Feedback (I am eighteen)*

Three weeks before you left, the woman who told you that we shouldn't be speaking past the hour made a complaint to the counselling service. *Iris was talking with a student around 9 p.m.* She had seen us together near the café and thought we were spending too much time together. I saw the report eventually and it said we were holding hands. Were we? I don't remember. We did sometimes.

When you told me about it you laughed.

*She's really crazy,* you said. *I think she's complained about colleagues before.*

I was mortified. I stopped going to the office on Mondays. I felt starving for you.

You said, *I remember cheating on my Spanish test in first grade.*

You said, *Why was I doing that?*

You said, *Have I always been this way?*

I said nothing.

*Why are we all so self-conscious? I'm afraid of never being loved, but is that what we're all like?*

*I mean, I am,* I said.

*But is it just us?*

When I got home that night, my mother seemed uncomfortable knowing I had been out with you.

*What could you and this woman possibly still have to talk about?* she asked me.

*We're just talking, I don't know.*

*We don't see you anymore because you're always out with her,* she said.

I bit the inside of my cheek and didn't try to come up with an explanation. I was glad she had noticed because it meant it wasn't all in my head.

*On Becoming an Adult (I am eighteen)*

Another night, two weeks before you left for California, we whispered in your room. Every few minutes you ran your hand through my hair.

*I'm so tired,* you said. *Sorry if I'm being candid.*

*I don't mind.*

*I'm so sick of my mom. We're all so selfish. Like,* all *of us.*

*I don't think so.* I only said that because at that moment I could have given you almost anything.

*We have to be. Everything is always about what we want. Don't you think?*

*Not always.*

*Sorry, I'm just feeling low.*

*You affect everyone so much,* I said.

*I've always felt like things couldn't be controlled.*

*So have I.*

*Do you think this is weird? Like, am I crossing lines?*

*No,* I said.

You had your hair in a side part that day, instead of pulled back. You were wearing a black dress and mascara. You had this way of veiling your eyes with unreadable emotion. Your beauty felt impossible. I wanted to write about it, but you were reading my diary so I couldn't. Time bore down on me while we lay on your duvet. The compulsion to kiss you, like the compulsion to speak with you, seemed like a law of nature. I wondered how this could be only an evening.

*I need to start taking responsibility for shit,* you said. *That's what it is after you turn eighteen.*

There was a pause. Everything in the air between us seemed to disappear and you looked at me like I was a child. You seemed afraid and stopped touching my face. It was a silence that ate up all the light.

*All right*, you said. *I should sleep.*

But we were ravenous. While I put my shoes on, we started talking again, and spoke for another hour sitting in the stairway that led down to the street, whispering so we wouldn't wake up your neighbours.

I was wearing a T-shirt that was cropped in the front. Before I left, you looked at my stomach, very slowly.

*On Reason (I am eighteen)*

While the time we still had disappeared, I wondered if the world would exist after you left. I was so elated with fear I felt like I could slip off the earth. I imagined futures in which we met by grey trees and watched the sky. Maybe Oregon. Somewhere.

*You don't always make sense, but I like it,* you said. *I wish I had more time.*

*What don't you understand?*

*Can I walk you home and tell you about it?*

*Yeah.*

I realized nothing would replace you. We walked home, ten kilometres, like we had months. We talked on my doorstep for an hour with our knees touching. You put your hand on my thigh and told me parts of me didn't fit together. You were so close to me by then that I think you may have started to realize something was wrong with me. Of course, I don't know that for sure. But it seems possible you might have started to hit on the inconsistencies that all of the doctors missed; there were parts of the world you completely ignored, but those kinds of discrepancies were within the parts of life you paid vigorous attention to. After you listed all the contradictions you'd noticed in me, I tried to spit up explanations, although eventually I realized that the things you didn't understand about me (was I faking being so forgetful?) could only be explained by the fact that I was so mentally ill.

With you, the world seemed like it was on the brink of fire. I was always choking it back, holding it behind my eyes. Every day in the last weeks, we lay in your bed; you played with my hair. You looked at me. We kissed the day after you walked me home, and I felt your hand push into my back. Afterwards you smiled at me like you were a camp counsellor. You used a strange voice with me, like the voice you used to say, *Hey, I'm Iris,* when I first met you. When I got home I threw up.

*On Morning (I am eighteen)*

I worked at a store in a mall that year. I finished my night shift at five in the morning and you were leaving the next week. I had a text from you.

*Want to talk?*

We whispered in your bed while the sun rose. You touched the side of my hand.

*There are so many things we still have on the list,* you said. *There are so many topics we haven't gotten to yet.*

*I know,* I said.

*I'm leaving soon.*

At eight in the morning I fell asleep in the hammock in your living room. Stephen made a comment to you about me sleeping over, but it didn't matter. We texted all day and met on the beach in the night. You didn't give me very good directions to where you were sitting. I wandered through the trees that enclosed the lakeside and saw you standing alone by the water. How did I always manage to find you, even in the dark?

*Stephen's being so condescending,* you said. *I told him to fuck off. I'm glad he at least has a girlfriend now.*

*I brought a list,* I said.

This list, like all our lists, like this story, was organized into subjects I wanted to speak with you about.

*On Remembering (I am eighteen)*

*Have you tried to kill yourself?* you asked me.

*No,* I said. *Have you?*

*Yeah. I've barely thought about it until now. I don't even think I've told anyone.*

Neither of us said anything for a long time.

You said, *I could talk to you for another ten hours.*

While we sat in the sand, I tried to recall how to get home, but my mental illness made it impossible to hold things together. Streets in my memory failed to coalesce into a predictable form. I walked home on the black roads and felt like the entire city was trembling.

*On the Yellow-Brown Grass (I am eighteen)*

The day before you left, I walked into the yellow-brown reeds by the lake. I felt bewildered, caught in smoke. The next day you would leave for California. I didn't know you would be there at the lake. The scene lingers in traces: my wish to avoid the east end, how I live in our last moment together like a house, the way yellow grass bends like it drank up too much of the earth.

The stalks of grass waited in columns. When you saw me you swore and you laughed. You kissed me so quickly I don't think you remember you did it. Your river of forgetfulness—which you live by, which you drink to survive—has a permanent flow. Never splitting, never draining into the sea, it ferries you only forward.

On that last night you named every star from your book and showed me that there is a crab beside Orion, to the right of his bow. If you name every star from your book, you have named every possible night. We spoke our dialect, calling out to parts of the world I can no longer name.

Perhaps I had to try to write it down for me to realize I'll never capture it, will I? For I don't think I've done it and I can't try again. This, my second attempt at the story, will be the last time I try to write about you.

Please keep reading. You know how we met, and how I fell in love with you. You need to see what happened next.

*On the End of October (I am eighteen)*

After you left for California, we texted all day, sent emails, and Skyped every night while you stayed with your family before starting your new job.

One evening you texted me, *I'm not even bothering to tell people about Toronto. It's too hard to explain different places.*

*I loved your email last night,* I said.

*Really? I thought it didn't make any sense.*

*No, it was like the beach.*

*Did not think it would be,* you said. *What are you doing right now?*

*Nothing, I'm looking at the houses on my street.*

*I need a break from my family. My brother's getting married. It's very different this year.*

*What do you mean?*

*I feel like I was in a different city with you,* I said. *It feels really unnatural to be at home right now.*

*I feel that way too. Trying not to forget all the stuff I promised I would change. In California. Honestly, I just want to be in love and have a baby.*

*I don't know what I want right now,* I said.

*What are you thinking about?*

You. I was only thinking about you. There was no room to think about anything else.

You said, *Want to talk tonight?*

Everything outside was silent.

Even on Skype, the way you moved your eyes made it hard for me to breathe. I looked at the image and longed, and longed, and longed. We spoke until two in the morning. I was nowhere. You were further on.

*On Cycles (I am eighteen)*

This terrible sickness has made me know I own nothing. Slivers of feeling, or ability, can always depart. I was never completely foolish, always knew in a way you would leave me, but in the three weeks after you left the city, I seemed to live the beginning of a life in which I could carry you with me. You were still my guide. My visitor, who brought me good and terrible things.

On the last day we spoke, it was hot for October. All day I could not bear to look at the sun, even in the periphery of my eye. I was still in the circle of your universe. Our symmetry bore into me. When we ended a Skype call that morning, I seemed to shrink into nothing because you couldn't see me.

*Why are you still speaking with this woman?* my mother asked me in the kitchen.

*We're really good friends.*

*Doesn't she have someone her own age to talk to?*

Suddenly I wanted nothing more than to talk to my mother about it. But I couldn't. Everything you told me you asked me to keep secret.

Then, in a text you said, *My mom is upset that I'm talking to you.*

I said, *Weird.*

*She never believed in hell until I came out,* you said. *And then she believed I was going there.*

I missed you rocking side to side in the hammock in your living room while I sat beside you. I missed feeling your ribs press into my knees. I sat in my room aching for you. Slices of clementine spread themselves over a dish.

And then, five minutes later, in the middle of a conversation about figure skating: you vanished.

*On the Rain (I am eighteen)*

Our world died so slowly. While it collapsed, I reached for its sun; still air split into high winds. When I met you I felt love overturn my shame, so that it seemed tiny. But your shame, whatever vanished you, seared everything in fire.

The gods loved me again, until they didn't.

We are barred entry to certain parts of the earth; I know this. We can't go everywhere. But why did you stop speaking with me?

*On Carelessness (I am eighteen)*

You left me as thoughtlessly as you did anything. I would have liked to think grief played a role, that you mulled over my image, reasoned a little with God. But no such thing happened.

You were in the living room with your mother and laughed at what I texted you. Maybe the TV was on in the background. You told her you were talking to me and she asked you why you were texting a student. She was the only person in the world who had the power to mortify you. So you turned me into dust in your head.

The jolt of being loved by you seemed to reassemble me for extraordinary use. It seemed by design. But there was no purpose. After you vanished, I looked for a secret. I navigated your various selves, tried to hold them to the light. Your hidden source, your explanation, turned into vapour each time I threw my arms around it.

You wouldn't swear a thing or make a promise, never compromised your future with a serious plan. But conversations with the beloved *do not simply end.* For you, the implications were puny. *For me, they play out.* As I said, after sickness, you were the second tear in my universe.

*On the History of Sound (I am eighteen)*

The day after you stopped speaking to me, I seemed to hear everything, the strum of the wind on a telephone wire or roots winding into the soil. *I hear it,* I thought, watching fog lift into the air. Every moment I looked over my shoulder to see you. The heat drained out of the world.

Today I remember so much of you only in sound. Why were so many of our conversations in the dark? Was it so you'd be less ashamed? Was it to prevent me from forming you into something complete? You were always further on. Is the feeling in my memory the flap of the wind? Or were you so close that it was your breath?

*On the Silent (I am eighteen)*

Taking note from the history of people like us, I didn't tell anyone that you had stopped speaking to me. I lived in the first lie you told me, that once I confessed to those in my life—*came out*, as they say—I'd be happy. I wasn't happy at all. When my hand accidentally brushed my friend's hand, a wave of fear ran through me.

In the weeks after you disappeared, young children suddenly seemed to be evidence of love. Couples with babies were alarming. You had left me nothing; our archive doesn't tell any story. Your presence had taken up the empty space in me created by mental illness, and after *you* vanished, nothing rushed in to fill this vacancy. It felt so credible that nothing had happened between us. All I had left of you was the red T-shirt you gave me, our emails, and hunger that rose and rose.

*On Ghosts (I am eighteen)*

Your memory was a second skin. In the months after you disappeared, I saw you in places like: the expressions of others, the glow of flowers in water, across the lake in a kayak.

You were in a different country, but I dressed in case I might see you. I found myself sitting in ways that would provoke you to ask me what I was thinking. I made lists of things to tell you. I remembered the gold in your eyes and searched for it in the faces I saw. I thought about trying to meet someone my age, but I wanted more than a girlfriend. I wanted you and your worlds.

*On Privacy (I am eighteen)*

During our months together, there was a girl at the office who was supposed to speak with you after me. We always kept her waiting. One time you cancelled her session last-minute to walk me home. When I left I always rushed past her.

A few months after you left Toronto, I saw her in High Park.

She waved, standing a few feet away from where I was sitting on a bench, looking at my phone. We spoke for a minute, and then she said, *I was always wondering, why did your sessions with Iris always go overtime?*

I felt thrilled and embarrassed.

*I don't know,* I said. *There wasn't a specific reason or anything.*

*You always talked right till the hour. Usually there's a ten-minute break.*

She looked at me like she needed to know. She seemed to believe there was an explanation. But just like with everyone else, I didn't have one.

*I mean, we were just talking usually.*

I said nothing more. You'd asked me to keep silent about the things you told me. Something in her seemed angry.

I realized that from the perspective of everyone else, we seemed to have been simply in love.

*On Preservation*

I lived by your rules for years after you vanished. I kept your secrets, maintained to my friends and family that *Oh no, we were just friends,* while I was privately obsessed with trying to understand what had happened between us.

If you were to stare into my mind, at the stem of the organ—just over the spine—you are present there, somewhere, in the ancient part. Your circular universe, which ends and begins forever, leaves behind traces in other worlds. Iris, you should know: the places you leave do not simply vanish.

I said I needed you to know what happened next. I might have lost myself in the symptoms of knowing you. You see, for a long time I worried that if I started to talk about you, I might never stop.

I need to tell you more about the state of madness I was in when you left me. For how can you know what I meant and what I did, when you don't know half of what happened to me? I am going to bring my sickness into the rest of the story I'm writing for you. I'll begin with a moment in the car, months after you disappeared.

*On Decay (I am eighteen)*

In March, four months after I stopped speaking with you, I said to my mother: *I feel like something is very wrong with me.* We were a little north of Toronto.

*What do you mean?*

*I don't know what anyone is talking about,* I told her. *I am empty. When I'm looking at a book, it's like I'm not looking at anything.*

I believe we were both certain that *something* was terribly wrong. But from this side, as I look at it now that I'm twenty-six, I think we set it aside with the other secrets that rest in plain view. From time to time, I grasped at it. But then I averted my gaze again, so I could live.

Later that spring, I saw an image of you online with your arm around a beautiful woman with light brown hair. I looked at the picture, and everything around my cellphone—the world—seemed to take on a secondary importance to the photo. I knew there was no picture of me that could elicit this reaction from you.

You left me in illness with a feeling of misshapenness. I always had the feeling I revitalized you. As you told your mother, helping me come out had been *fulfilling*.

I would like to tell you I'm healing now, at this moment. I have nearly everything back. But still, in the world we've made, sickness is a constricted life. One falls into habits. One enacts things that now have no function, no purpose, in health.

*On an Airport Hotel (I am nineteen)*

After about a year of silence, months after I said those things to my mother, you suddenly contacted me to say you had a layover in Toronto en route to visit a friend in Newfoundland. For three weeks, the only thing I did was believe that it might be possible that, when I saw you, you would end my complete bafflement about what had happened between us. You would say: *We were in love,* or maybe, *I'm sorry.*

I met you at the airport hotel, in your room. You hugged me. And you spoke to me like I was a child.

*Are you ready for college?* you asked.

*I'm terrified.*

*It's a big transition.*

But then after a while we returned to our dialect, the one we spoke in the sand. It felt like singing. You told me you would hire me next summer to work in Colorado, if I wanted to work outside. I have no idea if you meant it. What if I had spent even more years trapped by you?

*Are you happy?* you said.

*Yes,* I lied.

*Good.*

*Are you?*

*Yes.*

But were you? You were still dating the woman with brown hair from the photo. She was one of your colleagues and she had only had boyfriends until she met you. But you were scared it was falling apart.

*What are you thinking about?* you asked.

When I met you I felt brimming with thoughts. But I suddenly felt I had nothing.

*I'm afraid,* I said.

I had a real diary by then. It wasn't for you. It had secrets.

But of course to you these were the worst things in the world.

*Can I see what you've been writing?* you asked me. You stretched your hand out before I said yes, like you would in the coffee shop.

Everything seemed to pause. You would hate me for saying no or hate me when you read it. It was full of the things I had worked desperately to hide from you: full of confessions related to my fear that something within me had vanished. I handed it to you.

You read something along the lines of *I feel like I'm faking everything. I feel like I'm lying all the time. I'm not trying. I'm pretending about everything.* I was describing the atypical depression, it turns out. I was describing the life of a young woman without a mind.

*Are you going to live your whole life like that?* you asked. You looked at me strangely. And then, saying nothing else, you went to bed.

I wasn't sleeping well at the time. But that night I didn't sleep at all. You lay beside me, and I desperately wanted you to wake up. I needed to speak with you! I needed to explain! I needed to write you a diary entry you'd love, in which I wrote as a person who did not conceal anything. The whole purpose of sharing the entries with you was to perform your favourite thing: the act of hiding nothing.

But you kept sleeping; as always, you were further on.

I didn't mean to spoil everything, to throw it away. Our time together was an acrobatic feat, demanding painstaking care. At that point in my life I couldn't trust myself not to do things that were possible to do. I've often thought it was irresistible. But then again, I think it might have simply been the gods. Simply an error I made not to close the bathroom door when I went in at three in the morning to sob.

When I realized my mistake I lay beside you again. I'm sure you were only pretending to sleep. I wonder if then you realized you might have mistreated me. I wish that's what it had been. But I think you left quickly because you were simply embarrassed.

And beyond a curt message about a year later, our contact was over.

*On Being Missed (I am nineteen)*

You returned to living in transience: always in a state of motion, between temporary residences. While we were following each other online, it seemed like you were still living that way. Your online profiles dispatched messages of remembrance. From afar I watched everyone tell you, *I miss you,* as you left behind past after past: you lived in several states in the Midwest, Australia, returned to California, and left again to stay in New Zealand. I don't even know where you are today. But I still believe it is an extraordinary life. I don't mean to say it is better or worse than mine. Maybe I should move every year too and burn out prior selves.

I went to university when I was nineteen. I fell in love again, and again. But your nearness astounded me: time after time I peered behind things and found you there. I felt permanently tied to you. I thought we were the same woman. The enormity of loving you *loomed*, spread out in the colour of the sky. The whole world said your name in a chorus.

For a long while I assumed I would see you again. I thought all this gathering I'd done of the universe would *come* to something. I felt thankful for what you had given me, because you helped me learn to live the way people like us must live. In one way, when you helped me come out so diligently, so thoughtfully, you moved me forward by years with my life. But in another way, you trapped me, sealing me in a chamber by the water. You made sure I'd be nowhere for years, stuck longing for the things I believed, at that time, should have been ours.

Thinking the way I loved you was the way to love everything, I was careful, so careful, with lovers. I thought love was a stage play, carefully crafted. I thought it was so delicate that a careless moment, an open door, could vanish it like a young woman's mind.

*On the Strange (I am nineteen)*

The summer after my first year at university, my therapist said, *It sounds like she was in love with you.*

*I think I was in love with her and she didn't see it that way.*

*Why did she want to talk to you at five in the morning? Why did she want to read everything in your diary?*

*I don't know,* I said. *I don't understand it.*

*So you never told anyone?*

*Not for more than a year.*

*How come?*

*I couldn't find a word for it,* I said. *I didn't know how to say what I meant.*

I thought about the girl in High Park who had confronted me about you a few months after you left Toronto, and I imagined her and the therapist watching us talking from high above, presuming we were lovers. It was around this time that I finally became bored of wondering all day if you had been in love with me. I became more interested in what exactly you had done to me. And also, slowly, my madness became truly impossible.

*On the Carnival (I am twenty)*

My first serious girlfriend, B., was lovely. She sang and she knew how to draw. At some point I told her about you. Still, it was hard to put into words.

*Is that why you're so careful?* she asked me.

*What do you mean?*

*You're always ready for something to happen.*

There you were. I kept finding you places.

*I don't think she would still be affecting me,* I said. *It's been two years. I was so embarrassed about it for a while, though, since she was so much older. And I still don't even know what happened between us.*

*I remember I went with my family to a carnival, and my sister won a bear,* she said. *And I felt so embarrassed because she was younger than me and I didn't win anything. It's one of my clearest memories from childhood. Shame is so potent.*

*It's the most powerful feeling in the world.*

There were so many things in B.'s room. The Ikea spotlight, the white duvet, and the sketches on the wall were purposeful and had significance. I wasn't enough in the world to know what I wanted; I didn't know how to decorate a room. But things accumulated. Time rushed forward, even while I didn't have a mind. While it was with the dead, or wherever it was.

*On the Bridge (I am twenty)*

B. wrote me a song later that year that went *reset* at one part. The first time she played it for me, there was white light everywhere. Her hands had to move quickly to press all the right buttons on her computer. I felt a bit delirious. I knew the words were a little bit about you. I felt a dependency but a flatness at the same time. The song was like a conversation. The next verse was about becoming warm-blooded after swimming across a lake.

*On the Sick World (I am twenty-one)*

*How do you know what to like?* I asked B.

*What do you mean?* Her hair was in a high ponytail. She was sorting records into a pile to keep and a pile to sell. She knew exactly which ones to put where.

*Why are you keeping that one?* I said, pointing to a record with a purple cover. Her world seemed constituted by intuitions I could barely remember having. I was sad but intensely curious about what was happening.

*On One Thousand Stories (I am twenty-one)*

And as I entered my twenties, you should understand, the pain of having lost my mind had wound itself around me in so many circles, over the course of eight years, that I started to give way. I had been in contradiction with madness for too long. There needed to be a rupture.

Ending this sickness was how I began to free myself from you. It is not pleasant but here it is: I *loitered* in the world throughout the next few years, a little dead and a little alive. I would like you to know you can go missing within your own body. Everything can be within reach and not.

At times I felt nothing, but then the detachment would be displaced by a longing for my mind that had grown so violent I could not deny it was happening. I knew there was a terrible absence in me. When I looked at it honestly, its persistence challenged every logic I had been taught. It was a nothingness that was impossible to modify, that exertion in school and shifts in perspective could no longer conceal. It seemed as though you were simply a short distraction from sickness, and I would be stuck like this forever. I was running out of strategies to adapt to madness. I was running out of stories to tell myself night after night so I could survive.

I returned to experts, feeling more ferocious.

## *On Noncompliance (I am twenty-one)*

*I can't feel anything,* I told my doctor.

*How so?* he said.

*I used to like things,* I told him. *I liked history, soccer, reading, and movies. Now I don't like anything.*

*That's scary,* he said.

*I hear a ringing in my ears and it's getting louder,* I told him.

*That's mysterious.*

*I can't live like this,* I told him.

*I don't have a magic pill for this,* he said. *I'm not a magician.*

*What am I supposed to do?*

*Do you ever feel anything?*

*Sometimes a bit.*

*Well, why don't you appreciate that bit.*

He exchanged a look with the resident physician in the room.

*I'm twenty-one,* I told him. *Please tell me what I should do.*

He and the resident physician were in another world. They peered into mine and wanted to leave. They seemed to resist me. They seemed to find me offensive. The resident closed his binder like he had finished reading a story.

*On Living in the Present (I am twenty-one)*

I had to attend to everything so I would have something. Over the summer in Toronto I watched our lake water break over sand and wring it in mud. Fall yellowed the leaves, and I saw that when they shook in the air, the trees clung at them like mothers. When the only thing I did was exist, I had to be aware of the fact at every moment. It was a constant knowledge. *You* believed every whim that overtook you. I struggled to tease any out of the muck of my thought. Everything was just matter, maybe that is the way to put it. A book in my hands was dead.

Still, when I didn't care much about living anymore, there were hundreds more things I could do. I sometimes acted like I was deathless. This was the only thing I mourned about that time, because health brought along fear. Do you see?

One weekend while B. and I were walking down King Street holding hands, a young man yelled at us from a bar. He said, *Get a room.* It was very awkward. Things were so fragile between us then, the stability of our relationship was so subject to external events that intrusions like this could upset everything. I was sick at the time and didn't feel like I was in the world anyway, so it was very easy for me to tell him to fuck off. But the most recent time something like this happened, I was healthier and I couldn't bring myself to say anything. *What if he hurts me,* I thought, and I kept silent.

So this is a difference between the sick world and the healthy one.

## *On Reading, and the Content of Souls (I am twenty-one)*

One night at a bar a man said to me, *Reading is just part of my life.*

*What do you mean?*

*It's a fundamental part of who I am,* he said. *I can't live without it.*

In a way, sickness was having to pay attention. Nothing was simply itself. Things had an echo, demanded analysis. Everything was subject to change, to the fluctuations of dozens of mental states.

He seemed to think reading, and writing, could be intuited. He seemed to think they were things anyone could do if they tried. But what if he survived the destruction of his ability to love these things, like I had? He would still long for affection, for the love of certain women. Night would still eat up the light every evening, right in front of him.

## *On Palpitations*

In *intolerable circumstances,* the body eventually refuses to perform. When intense exertion fails, the body sometimes reasons it is best to play dead. That is what happened to me. After nine years of trying to force my way out of atypical depression through effort, I simply could not get out of bed.

I looked into psychiatric literature and tried to find an explanation. I told my parents, *I feel like I am one hundred years old.* I read about the golem, an artificial human from Hebrew mythology who steals the souls of the living so it can become alive again. I wondered if I was completely wrong about my understanding of the world and had actually been stolen away by a demon. I read about the "realm of the damaged gods," where people who realize their cultural myths are false go. Had I entered this dimension when I learned that hard work and focus did not lead to results in my case? Sustained by fear, I worked from my bedroom. One morning a clump of my hair fell out while I was brushing it.

Somehow, outside, plants were splitting through the soil.

*I would like to be interviewed on national television,* I thought. *I would like to warn girls what can happen.*

I tried to book an appointment with my psychiatrist that weekend, but he said he wouldn't see me for a few months. *There's nothing more I can do right now,* he said. In films, that is the thing the doctor says when the patient is approaching death.

## *On "Hills Like White Elephants" (I am twenty-one)*

*What's the problem?* said my professor.

*I can't do the work,* I said. *I've fallen behind.*

*Why?*

*I don't understand the readings.*

*They're difficult; it's normal to feel that way.*

*But I can't even understand the short stories.*

He looked at me and said, *Have you thought about going home?*

At home there would be the same problem. The problem was everywhere.

*I just need an extra week for this.*

*Fine, but I'm going to take off a full letter grade.*

The doctors didn't know what to do and neither did the professors. They didn't want to look at it. They wanted me to disappear. They only wanted to look at the students who could understand the short stories. I had been, in their eyes, somehow terminated.

The only thing to do was to lie around and try to do my readings. I focused on just one or two isolated sentences. In "Hills Like White Elephants," the woman said that once the world is taken away, you never get it back. The man said, "But they haven't taken it away."

*On Organic Elasticity (I am twenty-one)*

I began to constantly long for my mother, even when I was around her. I realized I missed something related to her that she wasn't.

*My professor suggested I go home,* I said on the phone.

*Do you want to do that?* she asked.

*No.*

I felt something extremely primitive. It was maybe just a need to make amends. A trail of ants on the balcony made its way toward the park behind the apartment I was renting with my roommates. It was getting colder.

"There is a compulsion inherent in organic life to restore an earlier state of things which the living entity has been obliged to abandon," said one sentence from my readings.

*On Punishment*

Your mother said we were going to hell. I didn't believe her but in this time I dreamt about it. There were rivers in hell. It had a geography and nothing was in proportion. Strange forces withstood destruction and waited. Some nights hell was flat, and other nights it was a spiral, bending deeper under the world so the greatest evildoers can be held in the most remote location. When I first saw you sin, when I first saw you envy me, I started to love you.

During this time I got the feeling that some people like us have, a terrible feeling that should take a life to attain: I felt a little damned. Too many people believed it for it to be resisted completely.

*On Touring Eastern Europe (I am twenty-one)*

The year I was twenty-one, I moved closer to giving up. You and I talked about the feeling of facing death together some nights, though always like we were promising it wouldn't happen in the future. But slowly the desire to end it all crept into things.

One can only attend to matter for so long. At a point, one tires of trying to bring it to life.

Like smoke, I began to relent; a fracture was imminent. It was more though. I wanted to destroy the terrible knowledge that this could happen. I wanted to drain all the lake water into the earth. I became desperate. It was a feeling of total entrapment.

During these months, while I went to class and tried to exist, I thought a lot about my grandfather's sisters who died in the war. I looked into their history and I thought, *I am sorry for giving up.* I had always been told that I looked like them but at this time noticed it was not just our eyes, that our jawlines bent in the same way and our ears were set at the same angle.

One afternoon I found an online tourist brochure that showed all the things there were to do in Uzhhorod, a city once in Czechoslovakia but now in Ukraine. There was a Jewish graveyard in the mountains just west of the city that the pamphlet named "abandoned." The site contained the graves of the Jews of Uzhhorod up until 1944, after which there was no one left to die. Linked to nature still, in the image in the pamphlet lilies had swallowed up some of the cemetery. Tombstones peered out of the soil, like breaths pressing into the wind. The earth sighed.

*On Change (I am twenty-one)*

The first rupture of my universe was sickness and the second was meeting you. The third rupture was health.

There have been others since. But they are meant for other stories, for different people.

When I was twenty-one, because of my depression, I had not really felt the heat or the cold in nine years. My processing capacity had declined by 70 per cent. I could not properly read a book or enjoy a movie. Somehow, for years, I had been someone else. A sickness had created new life in me: the life of a woman without a mind.

If you want to know what this life is like, it is like living in hell.

By twenty-one, I was willing to wager anything to try to regain what I knew I had lost. I was willing to join the dead.

The pills I'd been prescribed were tiny and white. I was alone in my room. *They are not working,* I thought. *I need to do something new.*

I could hear my roommates laughing in the living room. They were playing an old record and they were moving through their lives. The world was still happening. The seasons were passing. How could I rejoin the flow?

I was supposed to take one of the pills, but that day I took two and went into the kitchen.

So I experimented on myself and tried to find my own solution. I tripled, quadrupled, combined doses of psychiatric drugs I'd been prescribed. I told no one. It seemed to not be happening, and yet it was the only thing happening in the world.

And then, suddenly, in a wave of grief, I began to heal.

*On a Mitzvah (I am twenty-one)*

The secret experiment was a success. It was as strange, as awful, as stunning, as the loss of my mind. From nothing, the world came back to me. From the land of the dead, from the soil that breeds yellow grass, *my mind began to return.*

*On Firsts (I am twenty-one)*

The first thing I read after starting to heal was a book I'd been assigned years before, *The Lais of Marie de France.* A man jumps across the room to see the woman he loves. My mind held the narrative together. I didn't have to clutch it in a fist anymore. I could feel the structure of the story underwriting it, making it whole.

The first thing I wrote after starting to heal was an explanation for my madness that I could live with: a golem had indeed taken my mind, but in this case, it was just. For these golems were the unjustly dead. They deserved time in the land of the living.

*What if the place under the crust of the earth were the realm of the dead?* I wrote in my room, suddenly able to imagine again.

*Some underworlds from Greek and Yiddish mythology are not like heaven and hell,* I wrote. *They are places to wait in darkness inside the core of the planet. Perhaps the possession of my mind freed a few of the dead to escape this kind of an underworld and visit the land of the living. Couldn't it be that way?*

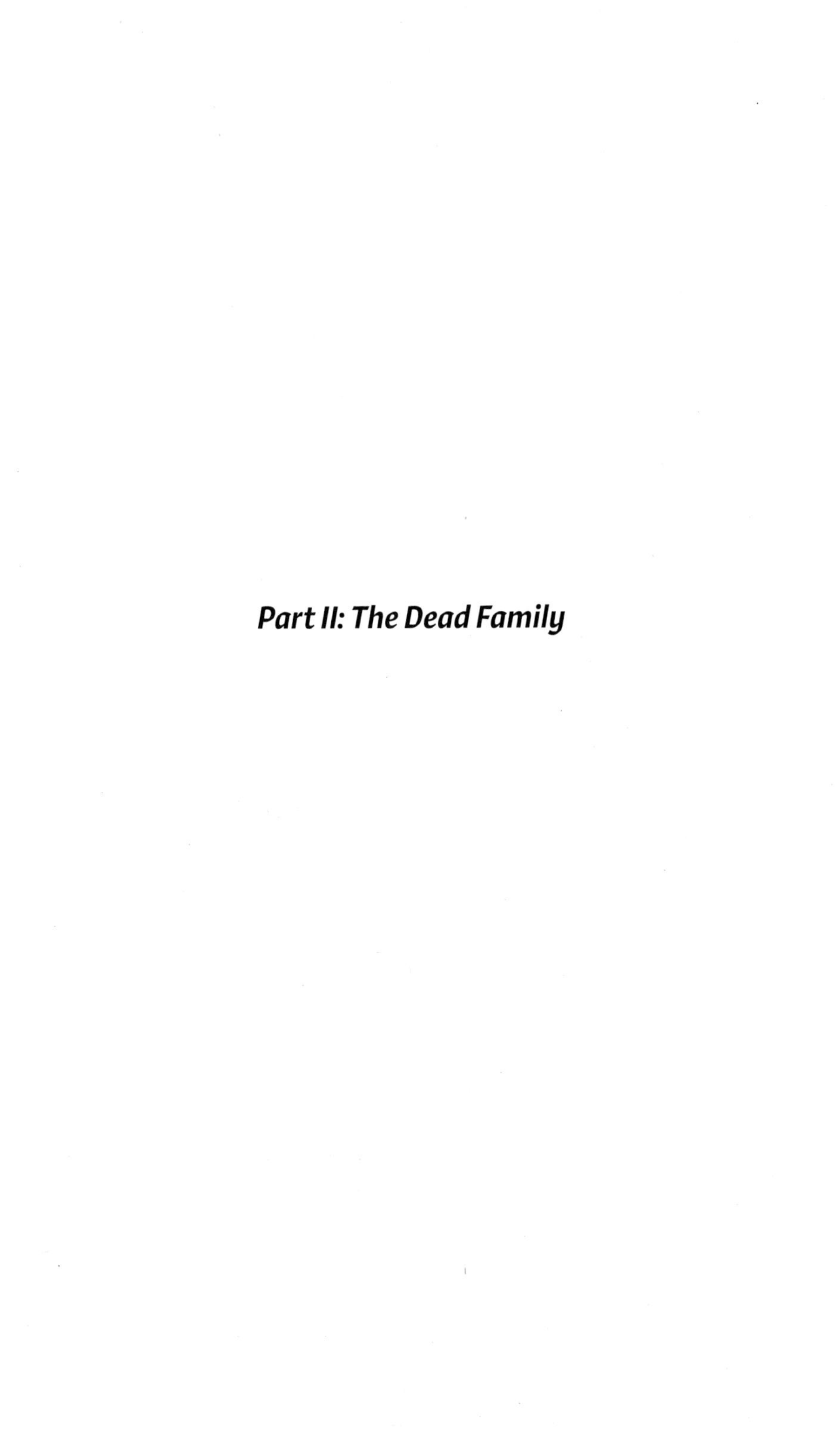

# *Part II: The Dead Family*

In the underworld, in a hearth, my great-grandmother Regina—who entered the world of the dead at fifty-three—sits in the middle of a circle of her children and burns meat for the goddess of silence, Mater Larum. The rite, as Ovid describes it, is intended to bring silence, muteness, for the benefit of the family. The offerings must move toward earth. In the underworld, this means they must rise upward.

The ritual is performed perfectly. Mater Larum is moved by the fragrance. She looks down and takes my mind. She brings it to the world of the shades and gives it to Regina. Grateful for the opportunity, Regina uses it to watch the sun burn over Budapest. Maybe afterwards she has dinner by the water. No one would reprimand her for this, for who would deny the dead a day of light?

Perhaps she passed the mind around. Maybe her children had the chance to use it to take things they wanted from the land of the living.

An exhale in a miserable part of the world. Grace for a moment. There is no logic in which this isn't just. The lucky deny the wretched exist, but they do. Forms of death abound, even in the land of the living. The gods love someone; then they love someone else.

The world of the dead is as different from waking life as dreaming is: an alien place. As the dead family immerse themselves into the land of the living, I recede into death's dimensions. Each skill lost to me is a skill gained by the dead. I forget; they remember. I trip; they regain the capacity for motion. I am gradually exiled; they return. I no longer need sweaters in October; goosebumps rise on their arms.

When minds vanish, they cannot go all at once. Instead, they change possession gradually. The dead family receive my mind from the goddess of silence in handfuls like it is yellow grass. They acquire it slowly, evading detection. What could be said to the dead to contest what they've done? If there is one mind and six people who need it, why should it not be divided among us?

## Their First Years in the Land of the Living

When the morning sky yawns, the mind, now a possession of the dead family, is put to use; it allows my great-grandmother Regina and her four children Joli, Rose, Leo, and Zoli to leave the underworld, giving them their just ration of experience in the land of the living. At first they can only do simple things. Together, they all watch the clouds. Regina's daughter Rose takes a walk. It is not so easy to wield the mind; it switches possession slowly and, anyway, there is no natural integration of a mind that is not one's own. But they adapt. They do more as they gather more of it, welcoming the alterations in consciousness and life force. Regina's son Leo exacts a powerful and awful revenge on an enemy.

The family of five seeks out different places, sees constellations wheel around the earth. Chances rain down. It is beyond their power to give back the mind. The loss of a mind, by their standard, is a puny evil. They desire time and now they have eternity, or at least as long as my mind sustains them. Like shadows they walk into houses that used to be stores, into the concert hall that was a shul, into a stolen printing press. They search for people who survived the war who look a little like them, who, protected by heaven, are still living in Uzhhorod. These people seem childish even in old age. Their beliefs, formed by their memories of luck and survival, lack the conviction that death can happen even to them.

The dead family write a series of notes full of anger. Their writing lacks coherence and suffers from tunnel vision because, at this point, they have not learned to use my mind properly.

It is only a twelve-year-old mind that they have taken, underdeveloped and constituted by adolescent rage. The primary desire of such a young mind is justice. And the primary desires of the dead are activity and expression.

Nor is it easy for the dead family to organize their memories. Cumulatively, they represent 167 years of life, and another 310 years of death. The thoughts and sensations overflow. Imagine trying to engage a twelve-year-old mind with this history.

So the dead family are only beginning to speak when they write, hastily:

*Don't think it was only loss! Our death was perfectly performed. There was something for them to collect.*

*We were not destroyed, we were purposefully transformed.*

*Look for what's left of us:*

*In the houses in Uzhhorod that were never returned*

*In the theft of our stories by villains for criminal purpose*

*In the money*

## Their Fourth Year in the Land of the Living

The dead adore my mind. Wishing to keep it for longer and gather up more of it, they burn oils, set up a conflagration while they sit in the palm of the world. Freed to roam in the daylight, the dead family become water and air. They cling to ship masts and oil rigs. They are not the gods of the sea. They are the sea.

In their fourth year in the land of the living, the dead chase away my final muse, stealing the last germ of psychic energy in my possession. At last, the mind is fully theirs.

Keen to dispute the belief among some of the living that there are things that are too terrible to occur, the family return to writing and begin to document the lost history of Uzhhorod. They want to make the knowledge that everything happens intelligible to the living. The mind provides the connective plasma, the stuff of argument and meaning. Without it, every image is discrete. With it, the images are harmonious and accumulative. Their writing is at last driven by life-giving movement, totally orderly.

The year I am sixteen I go to the beach, still without a mind. For the third or fourth time so far, the dead see me. While they watch me by the seaside, they think, *She is only a girl.* But some of the dead were only girls when things went wrong. Besides, promised decades of life, they have only had the mind for four years.

With their growing power, they take to everything: metallurgy, medicine, identifying the things with power on the human body. They construct a pulley, and a sphere that looks like the earth. They build a machine that lifts water, for drinking or for use as a weapon.

## Their Sixth Year in the Land of the Living

The dead family have three living descendants—me, my father, and my brother—all living in a house together in Toronto. They cannot help but notice strange things in their descendants as they wander the earth, performing activities.

These descendants do either nothing or everything. They have no time to sleep. They avoid block parties. Their fear is ravenous. As Regina counts petals, peering into the skin of the earth, she sees the descendants run circles.

"What are they doing?" she asks. Then one day she knows:

They are proving they would not have died like we did, in the concentration camps of the Third Reich.

They are proving that they are not us.

Over time, my great-grandmother Regina concludes that the living know half of the world, and only the simpler half.

Along with her children during their time in the land of the living, Regina has studied warfare and natural phenomena. She read an ancient Greek text called *On the Nature of the Child* and another called *On the Causes of Plants, On Stones.* But she has also been watching me, absorbing the consequences of the dead family's ritual. Regina has seen me chided by others because the ritual in the underworld stole my mind. The living believe what they experience is all there is, Regina observes, perturbed by their ignorance. The living abstract arbitrary things from their lives and assume they are true for everyone. They have lived in one world, one state, and disbelieve in the possibility of others. By the rules of their conscious life, they critique, even exile, one another. They do not understand that there are many things that go unnoticed while they are unviolated, Regina reflects. Not a single one of these strategies the living people deploy could cause the missing mind to return, because the mind has been taken by the gods. It is not possible to simply disown one's one mind. And yet, many in the land of the living believe this is the case!

These sorts of experiences slowly strengthen Regina's conviction that the history the dead family have begun to write is a pursuit of great importance, a pursuit to which they should dedicate themselves with singular focus. Their other activities are not as imperative. There is less need for the configuration of the atom. Clearly the living would greatly benefit from the written perspective of the dead, who have passed through the underworld. For the dead feel in a vast capacity: like easy instruments they respond to every touch. Even the busiest images can be enriched by the philosophies of death. The dead family can sculpt proper souls in this process of education, perhaps leaving the living with more wisdom.

*"Two worlds—the underworld and the land of the living—act onto the dead,"* Regina writes in the dead family's history, hoping it will encourage the living to heed their advice. *"We understand exactly what is happening to us."*

In the newspaper, there is a picture of the president of a powerful country visiting Uzhhorod.

"I feel that I am seeing upside down," Regina says to her children, showing them the newspaper. "The president's car is at the top of the image. His body hangs from his shoes, and he stretches his arm downward in a line. Underneath him is a white sky."

The mind the dead family have is a powerful thing. They have had it for six years, for half as long as its original owner did.

"Give up zoology and the selling of charms," Regina says. "There are things to say that only we can express."

"We could construct a temple, an architectural marvel..." says Rose, unsure if her mother is correct. "We could find a link between climate and medical affliction."

But Regina disagrees. She is certain they can improve the living people. "Temples house the dead. Medicine dissects us. But there are not many places to find the knowledge of the dead, which we can assemble in our book."

Hopeful, the family return to their text with these thoughts from Regina. They stop selling charms. They no longer practise geometry. Instead all they do is write, spinning every horizon in circles. They do not give back my mind, no matter how much I want it. They strike a meditative tone, a tone that is willing to teach. Their last name is Yiddish for writer. The Schreibers. It is all rather fitting.

## A First Excerpt from *The Book of the Dead*

The following is the passage they wrote that day, which was ultimately filed in the third volume of the history of the dead, "Visible Appearances," a shorter section describing a sequence of single days of significance to the Jews of Uzhhorod.

*On March 4, 1939.*

*In the morning, two hundred people glide over the path which marks the way to the cemetery. Like waves, the great mountains bear them up and down. Like shoals of fish, the people move as one creature. At the mouth of the valley, where the cemetery starts, they pause. Graves grip the soil like hands.*

*At the time this place, dressed in greens, had the power to tear at the sky. On these walks in the Carpathian Mountains, everybody believed in God.*

*In 1939 at eighty-six, Amalia Preust, an ordinary member of the community of the Jews of Uzhhorod, died of natural causes. This was while the site was still an anchorage for souls.*

## Their Seventh and Eighth Years in the Land of the Living

The five dead people complete the first volume of their history. Called *The Commencement of Time*, it covers the historic period spanning from the beginning of the world to the sixteenth century. They mention explicitly that

> *the beginnings of consciousness were very dangerous. Life had never been so fragile as it became once there was emotion. It was the mass sacrifice of silence, the kind known prior to sensation. (If a plant can be said to "know.")*
>
> *We all long a little for this time. Hence the feeling among some of us—based on nothing—that we were somehow better prior to birth.*

The dead set out to write the next three volumes of the history in Northern Italy, one of the places they had always wanted to visit. Throughout the journey they tangle themselves into the world.

*On we go,* they write, when they arrive.

*Never doubt the enemy's fear of the power of our desperation.*

*Never let them defame you with an apology intended to extinguish the rage of being entrapped.*

From the sky, the goddess of silence, Mater Larum, watches the dead family write. They will finish their history. It is only becoming more certain. The metals in the pulley they constructed rust. The link between climate and medical affliction—which it was within their power to uncover—remains hidden. Nothing disturbs their focus, not rain knocking at the window, nor the sighs of the girl whose mind they possess, nor the fact that Mater Larum can be moved by the fragrance, by the performance, of anyone's ritual, dead or alive. The goddess is really just an energy: something to be spurred on or repressed.

## Their Ninth Year in the Land of the Living

The mountains here rise and fall like lake water. The sky is white and wide. The winds, which have never been harnessed for human needs in this part of the world, race in circles. For nothing ends here. Things only churn.

A year of great significance has passed.

In the house they now occupy in Northern Italy, the dead family finish the fourth and final volume of the history of Uzhhorod while the past grows cold. By bringing so many memories of death to the land of the living, they have changed the universe permanently. They have produced the text they had dreamt they would! It is both compelling in its assertion of the validity of the knowledge of death and filled with ideas of the greatest consequence for the living. Masters of my mind, they have used it better than I ever did.

Regina sits in the sun, remembering the secrets of death.

*I am not Regina,* she thinks. *For Regina was alive.*

The dead sit together like fingers on a palm. At their centre is a knot. The earth boils beneath them, heating each country.

Rose and Regina sit by the water every evening. Commenting one night on misery, Rose says to Regina, "Nothing ended."

Regina says, "Things never ended," to her daughter.

They have observed the following while writing their history in the land of the living: Their descendants check twice before leaving home that the door is locked. The descendants believe they are living two lives, even three, for the ancestors whose names they carry. They craft systems of rules like they are building a world.

The women look at the same horizon. Wind troubles the ends of their hair. Monuments have been built for women who died like they did. Leaders of state mark anniversaries. Still, they see that in every corner of the world *the unspeakable* has simply continued to happen. Committed by everyone. The most terrible people persist in their passion for power, their beloved. Their machine hasn't faltered.

Regina returns to the first page the dead family wrote, when they had just received the mind. She makes an addition to their list.

*Look for what's left of us:*

*In the money*
*In the houses in Uzhhorod that were never returned*
*In the theft of stories by villains for criminal purpose*

*In what the descendants of all the dead did,* Regina writes. *In the heavens they made and the hells.*

And to finish *The Book of the Dead*, Regina writes a prologue.

*Our message to the descendants:*

*You see, we the dead have been on the wrong end of the machine.*

*We the dead know that a country is only a racket.*

*You can fool the living, but the dead do not believe they are safe. Nothing possesses the dead. They are not vulnerable to demons, nor to collective psychosis, nor to song. Let us give you an anthropology of life.*

The Book of the Dead *is not for all of the living. Let the ones who will listen read, the ones who aspire to the home of the gods in the visible skies.*

Rose asks if they chose the right god to court through their rites. She is not concerned for the girl whose mind they took, exactly. But the goddess of silence, of muteness, can only offer the dead the power to speak. Perhaps something more than speech was necessary to affect the people in the land of the living. Or perhaps the goddess, being from the underworld, did not mean well.

"No," says Regina. "It's not so. We can find justice through the rites. It's just a matter of utility. The gods can't be good or bad. They are energies: forces to accelerate or banish."

On earth I meddle with pills, and wait. A quarter of a human, I multiply the dose by four. I toy with self-sacrifice: it is an offering of life. I have gathered a holy spark.

And then, triggered by magic, the goddess of silence is moved once again. She reaches down and takes back the mind, my mind, as suddenly as she gave it away in the first place.

It is harmonious correction, inhale after exhale.

As Regina argued, they are simply universal laws: the propulsion of Regina's ritual is reversed by mine. Thankfully, *The Book of the Dead* is finished.

## Their Tenth Year in the Land of the Living

Leaves wind through the air and turn it red. Summer scatters, put to flight by the cold. Things repeat in a cycle, Regina sees. But they have imprints. They leave a trace.

The mind has begun to return. This is not because it is justly mine, or unjustly Regina's. It is what is happening. The mind is one of the things that should have been Regina's, and should have been mine too.

The dead family have been the sea. They spent years in Italy. They have completed a history; they saw terrible things. There was not enough time.

## Their Eleventh and Twelfth Years in the Land of the Living

The mind drains out of the dead family, stirring the vapour in the sky. The mind drifts by gazing faces. Currents of air bear it up and down. When it roosts back in me, the world starts to seep through it. It comes in pieces. It takes five years to heal.

The dead begin to misplace things. The winter cold is not so biting. They ride from Italy in chariots while they wait for the mind to vanish. The chariot wheels, the liveliest things in the world, rustle through grass and sand. The dead family cannot be controlled from within. They do not cling to the land of the living. Instead, they drive the chariots north, to their home in Uzhhorod. They do not recall their memories of death so well anymore. The number of words they wield diminishes. They stop needing shoes to shield their feet from rough gravel.

The dead cannot be enticed. There is nothing in the land of the living for the dead to mistake for a hiding spot that might conceal them so they can keep the mind forever. As Regina said, they know exactly what is happening to them.

## Their Thirteenth and Fourteenth Years in the Land of the Living

From the south, in a sea cave, the dead family watch the mind disappear. In their last year, they make a second copy of *The Book of the Dead* to take with them back to the underworld. The text was written for the living but perhaps could serve the dead as well. They're tired and hungry. In many ways, the land of the living has repulsed them. They know it cannot be fixed by a single book.

It was worth it, however, to come back a little from the dead. Not for everyone. Not for all families. For them, though, they have had daylight, that thing that everything craves. Their ritual was a success: it has benefited the family. Couldn't it be that simple? That one could come back from death and enjoy it?

## A Final Excerpt from *The Book of the Dead*

It is possible you will find *The Book of the Dead*. If you do, here is what you will read on the first page of Chapter I:

> *Our history begins in earnest in the sixteenth century in Uzhhorod, with the construction of the Jewish quarter. We name the lives which passed through it, passengers who moved at a steady pace until the war. Afterwards we lay out a long history of death, tracing the development of the false theory of living which persists in some minds. Our next histories take from experience. We reveal the way of seeing shared by the dead. We include a history which binds together three mornings, in particular three dawns. (Three is a divine number, signifying the beginning, the middle, and the end.) At the end of this volume, we propose the sky never weeps.*
> *Indeed, it is only the human face which truly sobs.*
>
> *While you read, perhaps remember:*
>
> *Every mind is a world. When a mind is lost, sadly a world dies with it.*
>
> *All idols are false. Press a little on any idol, and it folds.*

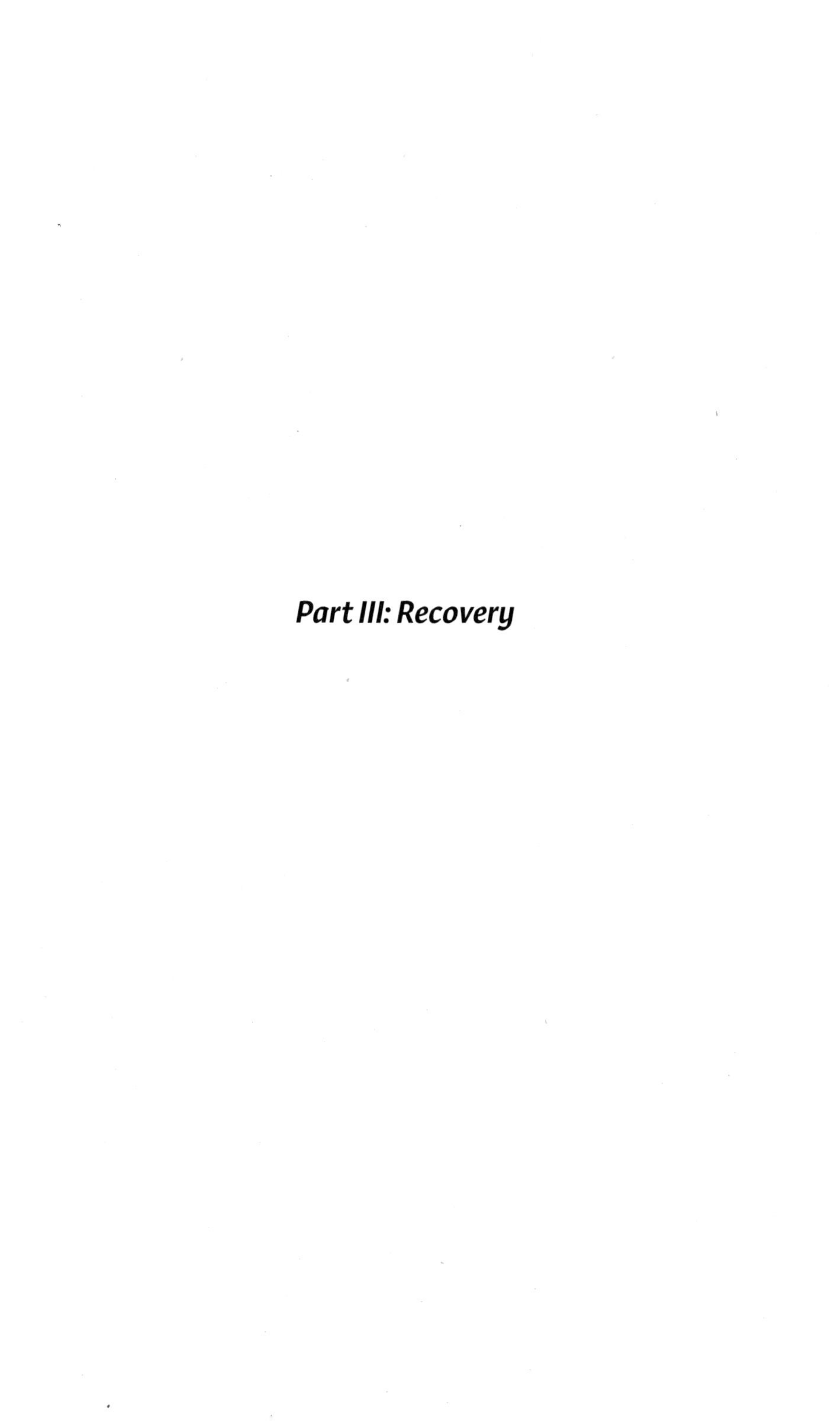

# *Part III: Recovery*

*On Ending a Family*

Two nights ago I dreamt I had a baby. I worried for it. I tried to think about this book, but all I could think about was the baby's hand, in which the world seemed to be folded.

I don't know if I can have a baby. I have been told I shouldn't. People have said this to me because this sickness has no merit. It is the inability to feel. Besides the carelessness, it gave me nothing, only took took took so that I was a thing that diminished. And the trauma of the sickness *still* invents me. Its apparatus seems endless.

But then again, maybe there are things I could protect a child from.

As I said earlier, I sometimes wonder if this sickness was caused by a relative's life in the war. The knowledge that all things happen, it seems, might be passed along in secret. Are we destined in a wave to live these things out forever? And when I'm told not to have a child, would they like me to end my family line?

*On the Genius of Forgetting*

Perhaps one day, somehow, I'll find some other way to stamp out this disease. "Resilience," which the lucky try to tell the unlucky about, is said to be this by psychologists. It is interception; it is the end of habits and the repetition of trauma. It is finality as creation.

*On the Annual Check-In (I am twenty-two)*

When I told my psychiatrist I had found a cure for my sickness
and re-entered the world, he said he was happy for me.
    *What did you do to cure it?*
    *I quadrupled my doses,* I said.
    *You shouldn't do that,* he said. *It's very dangerous.*

*On the Eccentric Circle (I am twenty-two)*

As my madness lifted, Iris faded from me into a mist. But I didn't know if there was a world to move forward into. Where was I going to go? Back into the world that had wanted me to disappear? To do this contradicted all of my strongest instincts. If I immersed myself alongside the people who had sent me away, I would probably have to re-enter their consensus about reality. To be with them I would have to pretend I had never lived behind a boundary between myself and everything else. I suspected that if I re-entered the old world I would have to ignore all the other dimensions I knew of, that I could keep very little of what I learned, which I regarded as astonishing, terrible knowledge.

But the stories that Iris told me—that we were just friends, that she hadn't done anything wrong—lessened their grip on me as time passed. Because I was recovering, I began to see all the old things differently. It was hard at first, but like the dead I practised using my mind, and I became better at it. I saw the way Iris and I were lovers. I began to tease out the nature of her mistakes; from my viewpoint of partial sanity, slowly, I clarified uninterrogated parts of the past. My mind subverted old images. I was able to start to reframe it all. I don't know when she truly left me. Maybe she still hasn't. Because although I hate her, I am tenderness for her still. I still want to gather her, hold her. In a way, she helped to create me. Perhaps in a few years I will go *Aha!* and realize she is gone. I won't write to tell her.

*On Testimonials (I am twenty-two)*

The loss of ten years to madness was menacing. There was nothing greater. I became increasingly sure about what had happened to me, but no one else knew. It sounded absurd to say it out loud.

*It seems like I've been extremely depressed for ten years,* I told B. when we caught up.

*Don't you think you could just be projecting?*

*No, definitely not,* I said. *I'm getting everything back, day by day. Every few months I improve a bit. And I can catch stuff that's thrown at me again.*

*Wow.*

What else was she supposed to say?

*I think I've been depressed since Grade 7.*

*That seems possible,* said my mother.

*I think I'm getting better now.*

## *On a Long Time Away*

I sometimes feel a little like I have come back from death. An undiagnosed sickness is terrible trauma. Its flashbacks, its nightmares are lifelong, because a sick human mind is a little reptilian. Its ancient part is too powerful and overwhelms the more historically recent rational parts of the brain. The reptilian mind is white-hot and fire-like. It groans if it is not properly restrained.

I cannot find the word for it. I hope I will one day. My horizon seems so strange.

I stopped needing to tie my keys to my bag. I could notice the difference between sweet and salty food. I could tell if a piece of fruit was fresh or old. Mosquito bites became very intrusive. The comments people make—their stream of observations about the immediate circumstances—were sensible suddenly, and I started to make these kinds of comments too. We were living in them together. *Yes, it is very humid. Yes, the keyboardist was bad. No, I don't think I can get there in time either.*

A great and long sickness leaves the patient with the understanding of change. The knowledge of sickness is as long as the knowledge of love.

*On Trivia (I am twenty-three)*

People asked me questions I couldn't answer.

Do you like summer? *I don't know.*

Are you late to appointments? *I don't know.*

Do you care if things are clean? *I don't know.*

What were you like as a teenager? *I don't know.*

You've grown as a writer. *I think my mind returned, and that is all that happened.*

Are you sensitive to pain? *I don't know.*

Do you get cold easily? *I don't know.*

Do you like surprises? *I don't know.*

You've become a lot more present. *I think my mind returned, and that is all that happened.*

You seem well. *I think my mind returned, and that is all that happened.*

*On a Ladder (I am twenty-three)*

I started to do things again. I got a research job in Toronto and wrote a research paper.

Everyone at the job was nice to me, but I was extremely distrustful of them. Every conversation played out against how it would have gone if I hadn't gotten better. Here was the thing: expert opinion had failed me again and again when I was sick. My own volition was the only thing I had relied on for years.

*This is excellent,* said my boss. *I like what you did with it.*

I went home feeling very still. The sun was growing lifeless. I felt that I knew my supervisor's secret. I knew that if I had still been sick, she would want me to disappear. I knew that a workplace network was a bargain, not a friendship.

I was terrified of getting a concussion and causing the depression to get worse.

Suddenly, I was afraid of dying. I was less open to the world. I wouldn't risk losing myself on a whim, because I had become protective. I had things that could vanish.

I stopped riding bicycles. I lost interest in dangerous activities and large crowds. All I wanted to do was preserve the health I had resurrected like a temple priest, like the *magician* my doctor told me he wasn't. I didn't feel that my body could handle any external disturbance. I watched out for threats with vigilance and stared at the orange stars in relief.

*On Hunger (I am twenty-three)*

I woke up after a date the summer I turned twenty-three and got on the streetcar. The air was very hot. The sun was so bright I felt overwhelmed by the knowledge of how things looked. Everything was opening.

I felt a strange kind of momentum. I knew I was exchanging worlds. The girl I'd gone on a date with the night before ran through my mind and I felt a hyperattunement to everything I had said. It was the kind of paranoia that precedes love, and constitutes it in some ways. She was surrounding me.

*Goodbye,* I thought, to Iris. I threw out my burdens. When I walked off the streetcar, the wind was soft. All the planets were hiding. The romance didn't last, but I felt so much hope. I loved her more than anybody else, and it killed Iris, in my head.

*On Daisy by Marc Jacobs (I am twenty-three)*

She came over to my parents' house while they were away, and we sat on the swing in the backyard. My cat narrowed her eyes.

*I miss my grandmother,* she said. *She bought me these shorts a few years ago.*

I could feel my head filling up with someone new. The idea of her flowed faster and faster. I was losing my footing. I was looking upward at something.

*This was the best night of my year,* she said after we slept together. The front hall smelled like her perfume. I didn't want to tell anyone about her because I didn't know how I would stop talking about her if I did.

I called my friend and said, *I am so in love I feel like my head is going to explode.*

*On Atonement (I am twenty-three)*

So on that day, five years ago now, I finally loved someone more than I loved Iris. I realized I was moving beyond her. But *still* I was performing the habits she taught me, speaking of everything but love, holding the relationship in order with an impenetrable grip. When I saw myself doing this, when I realized I was rehearsing something I learned for Iris, I emailed her. Without meditating on the details, I asked for an apology.

But when Iris emailed me back, she said she had no idea what I meant. I had to say it explicitly. I put it very clinically, but I did not say it all: *We were way too close, given the power differential inherent in a relationship between someone who is counselling someone else. It has continued to affect me.*

She wrote back about a week later. She apologized for *something*. Whatever it was, it wasn't what happened. She spoke in metaphor, said she had *crossed lines*. She said, *I was very young at the time,* although of course I was much younger.

Whatever she apologized for was a fraction of the thing, whatever part of it she was willing to see. So she didn't bother with atonement for all the things I was left with, for how I looked longingly at a kayaker who resembled her when I was twenty and thought, *Please take me away from here*. It scared me that twenty-seven seemed young to her, and I was afraid of forgiving her one day on that basis. When I saw her response, I knew I would have to write our story properly, soon. I knew I would try to say everything before too much time had passed. Here I am.

*On Café Libre (I am twenty-four)*

*That was excellent,* my dad said to me after I presented the research paper.

I didn't realize until that moment that I had hoped presenting the research paper would save me. I thought it would be an act of magic, something so precise it could have been restorative.

*I don't know what I thought was going to happen after this,* I said.

We went out for lunch with my grandmother. Water rose from a fountain outside the café window. Everything was organized.

*Order whatever you like,* my parents said. It was the kind of day that wouldn't have happened in the sick world.

Would my parents and I ever be able to forgive each other for what had happened? I wanted to try. I was starting to feel a kind of communion with my childhood self, or at least a relationship with her of some kind. Every moment of our lives until I became sick had told us to surrender to the beliefs of experts. Now a new world had asserted itself.

*I'm sorry,* my mother said to me, one afternoon in the car.

*On Orion (I am twenty-four)*

When I looked into a telescope a few months later, the words I said to my parents seemed to rise up the sky. We had driven to a dark-sky preserve in North Frontenac. On the drive up I asked them not to talk about what had happened when I was a teenager, and they listened to me.

The gods loved me again by that time. But I know they could forget me. Everything is possible, speakable and not.

My parents tried to light a fire that night, but wind caught the flame and it vanished. I felt so much better, but my mind was still splintered. Strange images came to me, dispatched by a force beyond my control. It takes a long time to adapt to the return of a mind. It is not a natural transition. Like a transplanted organ, the body's instinct is to reject it. Every flashback felt like a long sigh running through me. My mind struggled to retain its shape, showing me all the possible forms of life and death. Even at that point, two years into recovery at twenty-four, there was still the feeling that I could drift into it. That if I relented, I could depart.

*On Complex Presentations of Immunodeficiency*
*(I am twenty-four)*

My best friend from university, E., got sick. She was exhausted all the time and couldn't think. But she didn't have a proper name for what was happening to her, so the world progressed like nothing had happened. If she couldn't act well, the world wanted her to disappear.

It was a funny thing, putting it to language with someone else, particularly as I was slowly healing.

*They can't cope with it if it doesn't have an obvious cure,* I said.

*Well, what am I supposed to do? What happens to all of my potential?*

*I don't know,* I said. *Things are always changing though. Sometimes people just get better. Maybe it's about trial and error.*

*Why doesn't anyone believe me?* E. said.

*I feel like it's too tragic for lots of people to believe.*

That summer we rented an apartment together and tried to understand how our lives could be so good and so bad at the same time. It was my first try at letting people into the world of my depression.

*It's kind of like we were abducted,* I said.

*Yes,* she said. *But also evicted. They made examples of us.*

Sometimes we were angry, and other times we just talked about it. There are a million things to say about sickness. It is the most fruitful topic on earth, other than love.

Over those months, we faced something very fundamental

and hidden together. We sat around and wondered why we had been smited, or if we even had been. We tried to "get it together" and accept how much of the inner universe could be destroyed. How much loss could a lovely sunrise correct for? What about a colourful childhood memory?

*On Who Can Know (I am twenty-four)*

One afternoon that summer, I drove to my grandmother's apartment.

*When I was thirteen, I couldn't do my school work anymore,* my grandmother said after we ate lunch.

*What?* I asked her.

*I just couldn't do it. It took years before I could study again. I don't know what happened.*

I reeled with this, sitting quietly in her living room for a long time. I thought about my twelve-year-old self. I felt like I'd miscarried her. I knew I could never properly bring her back to life. I wondered what kind of life I would have in this new body, which I had created by refusing a cruel social destiny. I longed for how I saw the world before I got sick. Clouds outside the window arched into the sky.

After my grandmother said this to me, I thought it had to be a genetic problem. But now I wonder if it is just a shared disposition, a certain sensitivity to things. It's probably a bit of all the explanations I've dreamt up, although I wish there was something tangible to blame. Because it is probably more than a medical condition. Perhaps there are complexities at play around us we cannot fathom, and it hurts to think of it. Perhaps something really has stolen our minds when they vanish. The only solution I like is that we have given things to the dead.

*Why didn't you tell anyone about this?*

*I told everyone,* she said.

*There's so much in people that you see when you're like that,* she said.

Had there been a sickness stalking my family this whole time? There was nothing to consult. She could not direct me to any literature on the topic of what had happened to her. The things that happen to teenage girls are secrets. They are rarely recorded. Teenage girls cannot be witnesses. They are just watched.

*On "Lived Experience" (I am twenty-four)*

I stayed at the research job for years. The project I was working on was related to the sociology of medicine and how patients should be treated. I used my instincts to make suggestions.

*Your experience has made you very insightful,* my mother said.

*This is very good,* said my supervisor.

*Good things can come out of bad things,* said my therapist.

Nothing on this earth could ever make what had happened worth it. It was not worth it. I can only try to understand it. Trying to make it worth it was like trying to bring back the dead.

Instead, we must have a world where no one, no matter how sick they are, is made to disappear.

*On the Break (I am twenty-five)*

There was still something present connected to my sick self, but the people in my life were startled by how different I now was.

*You really used to be gone,* my mother said.

I began to put words to my time of silence. I spoke, louder and louder. I wanted to answer every question I had put to myself when I started to recover. It may take another story, but I have begun.

*We missed the depth of the situation,* said my father.

It was a tragic thing to reckon with. It was my turn to teach, my homecoming.

Nothing ends. I can revisit things too. I can rename things. These memories are deathless. They have no fixed fate.

*On a Gap (I am twenty-six)*

My mother's friend Michelle has a daughter who is eighteen. I talked to her briefly at dinner this summer. We were eating in the backyard. She was going to start university, but everything was a mess because of the pandemic. She didn't know what was going to happen.

She seemed so young. She had finished high school only a few months before. I thought about all the things I had done since I was her age. I thought about Iris suddenly and what she did.

Did you know I used to think I was Iris?

Wind passed through the grass. The trees looked like they were propping up the sky. I remembered how much Iris adored me and how she forgot me like it was the most natural thing in the world. I wrote once, *Let me grow to be unlike her,* and I meant it like a prayer. And now she had slipped from my hands while the world sank in.

In that moment, I knew the exact form of Iris's carelessness. I plotted out the precise difference in experience that had existed between us and tried to imagine being cruel enough to ignore it. I had asked and answered a thousand questions since I was eighteen. I had told and revised a thousand stories about myself and other people, and how nature works, and countries. Iris did too much and then lived as if nothing had happened. I had finished high school only a few months before we met.

The thing I recognized so much in her during our fall together was her sorrow. But I did not feel so sorrowful anymore.

*On Surprises (I am twenty-four)*

Later that summer, on the way to visit a friend, I walked down College Street. By the curb, outside Iris's old apartment, was the hammock from her living room. What were the chances that I would walk by right when someone had put it out there?

It didn't look out of place outdoors, of course. I looked around to see if anyone was coming for it, but when I continued walking it was still there by the sidewalk.

When I got to my friend's apartment I told him about the hammock, and my autumn with Iris.

He said, *That's really fucked up.*

*Yeah.*

*What a strange story,* he said. *She sounds horrible, but I just love the story. I don't know why.*

*Yeah,* I said.

I wanted to say something more but I didn't know what. We were quiet.

*I was so scared I would never find someone who would want to talk to me that much,* I said. *I thought everything was over.*

*Why was she so interested in you?*

*I don't know. Looking at it from this side, it seems different. It was a long time ago, I guess.*

*Do you know what she's doing now?*

*I don't really know,* I said. *I feel like she's in the same world. She's passing through places. She's very good at meeting people. I'm getting so close to the age she was when we knew each other, but she's in her mid-thirties now, I guess.*

*It seems really unfair.*

*It was,* I said. *You can really take someone over by helping them in a certain way.*

But still, I felt well. I had the whole world. I was healing every day and I could see every hue of the afternoon.

*On Pebbles, Heaven, and What's Between*

When I was sick, all I could do was give names to things, because I seemed unable to access anything outside of myself. But now I am renaming everything. I believe it is the greatest power. I will choose what I mean by love. I will gather it as I want to. And if naming is our most perfect habit, you cannot interfere in how someone speaks of the world. You cannot distort their sight. I can take any memory and name it, forever.

Even if no one knows what I mean, I will claim meanings for things. I will say what is violation. I will say what is love.

*On All the Universes*

I wrote this knowing things were pressed for time. I needed to write while I was nearly the age Iris was during the autumn we knew each other. I needed to write about her while I could finally say it, now that I finally understand what had happened to me. I wanted to set down the things I kept from her and the things I had learned since. I thought it had to be while I was fresh from sickness, while I was fresh from longing for her like she was something they stole. While I could still remember the dream I used to have about her, where she ignores me while wind turns the sky into mud.

When we were together, the lake seemed to sing the notes of a command. I started to think there were things the air couldn't take. I wanted *fluency* when I fell in love with her. I wanted to be able to speak again.

But she didn't hate secrets. They were her craft. She held them herself and she gave them to others. Now that I'm nearly the age she was, I can look at what she did and know its shape. I finally know the form of what she didn't mind maligning. Every concern she partook in that exceeded my experience weighted the scales in her favour. She became Fortune, and that is no one's right.

In every possible world, when offered what she offered me, I say yes. In none do I say, *Why?*

For so long I thought things were my fault; I felt ridiculous. For so long I wondered, *Did I do all this or did she?*

But it was not my fault. I shouldn't have beheld love like it unhatched moments before because it is ancient, and she misled me. She gave me a shadow. She compelled me to see her as she wanted me to, and it was easy because I was sick. I acted against nature, against time, to try to keep her.

Trauma inoculates the reptilian brain. Here she is. This is violation, something that is unjust by every philosophy.

I am fateless, and she made me believe she was the call of my fate. Love is not contingent on her.

Iris, love is old. Dante says, "Love is our common death." It is the energy that is the cause of motion, which is the thing that leaves a trace.

*I've rewritten most of the story,* I told my mother. *There is still more to say. It's my last chance, I believe, to say some of these things.*

*It has to be better than the story that disappeared,* I explained. *Or I'll be too upset that I lost it.*

I leaned into the wall. It was evening. The story was not what it should have been. Should it have been longer? Should it have been an essay? Should I have recorded every word said between us? I thought about the things we said to each other that I hadn't included.

Maybe I had forgotten something essential from the first story, the story that vanished. Or maybe the answer was somewhere else before me.

I wondered, *Is there no way to redress things? Is there no world to build?*

I wanted to tell the story again in a thousand worlds. I wanted to retell it until I could say to my mother, *Now I am glad about everything.*

I realized I could not make things magnificent. I realized I would live with things as they were.

*On Harmony (I am twenty-six)*

The winter I was twenty-six, I fell in love for the first time in a way that didn't feel disordering.

*You are all the things I've liked the most about all the best people I've met,* I said at my apartment.

Everything was so still that I went back to my parents' house and started writing the first story for Iris in a blue journal, the one that I can only remember small parts of now, that was much angrier, more experimental, and went missing during a move.

Now that I am much better, I am instructed to work even more. I am encouraged to *make up for lost time.* I am told to *catch up on knowledge.* I wanted to say this in part because I think that I do know the world. That although I missed things, I gathered up other things. And perhaps I do not want to catch up with the old world, which told me I had no future if I was not a mother, which told me that if I could not work, I was wicked. Sickness and recovery have led me to lose faith in this world, which cares only for those who can repeat the same actions again and again and again at the right times. The contempt I experienced is still felt by others.

My experiment with medication might have not worked, or might have harmed me. As I said before, we need to build a world where no one is made to disappear. I will never be *healthy* anyhow. Always my mind, which vanished and reappeared, will exist adjacent to some of the ordinary things. I will feel like a bit of a stranger, with flashbacks and a funny sense of time, until I die.

But in another way I will never be unhappy again. The world regained is a different thing. I have been watching fall turn the leaves orange and red. Yesterday, when I paused at the top of a long staircase, a bit of sunlight fell in through the window. I swooned. It was all enough.

Everything sat in the fold of my palm.

*On Airs, Waters, Places (I am twenty-seven)*

On my twenty-seventh birthday I went swimming with my friends. I thought of Iris briefly. I was healed and I wasn't. I had nightmares from losing my mind. My mind had returned to me.

The birds sobbed. We walked on a path that wasn't a path, that was only a gap in the trees. The ferns threw black shadows. Water fell from tree branches in beats. I heard cars gliding toward the city.

I felt solitary, a perfect solitude. My mind seemed to be mine. I didn't share it with anybody. I felt further on.

I watched a bird fly up, pressing its head into the space between the heavens and the earth. It sang, *My oh my oh my oh my,* while it rose.

*On Waiting for a Lover in the Night (I am twenty-seven)*

Yesterday night I waited in silence. It was very dark. I felt strange, but I did not feel pulled by the loss of anything. I seemed to be under a sea.

The breath of the wind has a rhythm as long as the night. Earth has a history; yesterday night I felt like I could remember it all. I imagined all the times it had sighed, or retched. I saw the glow of its heat, climbing up from the underworld. I looked into all the noise, parsing through the history of sounds. *Maybe somebody somewhere remembers the word for the feeling of sickness,* I thought. *Perhaps these words have been said to somebody, at some time.*

But the truth is, we lack certain terms. If I can't find them, maybe I can create them. Maybe one day I will go *Aha* and write a new word myself.

Dried leaves were everywhere yesterday night, stirred and then left by the wind. Wouldn't there be snow soon? Wouldn't it spill out everywhere? The moon was so white. I wanted to write a history so I would not join the vanished things. I suddenly never wanted to die.

*The story is finished,* I told my mother today.

*Are you sure?* she asked me. *Is there something else you need to say?*

But I had written everything on the topic I was going to. I will be twenty-eight soon; I will be older than she was. There have been other ruptures I need to discuss. Although even these, in some way, were set into motion by the autumn I spent with Iris when I was eighteen.

## *Acknowledgements*

Thanks to Rachel Gerry for preliminary edits. As well, thanks to Catherine Gordon and Benja for early edits, advice, read-throughs, etc. Thank you to Malcolm Sutton for making the book (much) better, and to Hazel, Jay, Britt, and Reid at Book*hug Press.

## *About the Author*

MIRANDA SCHREIBER is a Toronto-based writer and researcher. Her work has appeared in places like the *Toronto Star*, the *Walrus*, the *Globe and Mail*, BBC, and the *National Post*. She has been nominated for a digital publishing award by the National Media Foundation and was the recipient of the Solidarity and Pride Champion Award from the Ontario Federation of Labour. *Iris and the Dead* is her debut book.

PHOTO: SARAH BODRI

Colophon

Manufactured as the first edition of
*Iris and the Dead*
in the spring of 2025 by Book*hug Press

Edited for the press by Malcolm Sutton
Copy-edited by Stuart Ross
Proofread by Laurie Siblock
Type + design by Malcolm Sutton

Printed in Canada

bookhugpress.ca